Banker's Friend

David Bowra

IGUANA

Publisher: Cheryl Hawley
Editor: Paula Chiarcos
Front cover design: Jonathan Relph

ISBN 978-1-77180-731-9 (paperback)
ISBN 978-1-77180-742-5 (hardcover)
ISBN 978-1-77180-730-2 (epub)

This is an original print edition of *Banker's Friend*.

Banker's Friend

For my sons, Christopher and Gareth. Follow your dreams.

Author's Note

This story is a work of fiction, loosely based on events that took place. Any characters with similarities to real people is an unintended coincidence.

Chapter 1

Vancouver
November 2000

The world is neither flat nor round, it's crooked.

—Justice Samuel Toy, British Columbia Supreme Court of Appeal.

Bob Stuart took a long hard look at himself in the mirror. He bent over the sink, splashed some water on his face and took his time drying it with a paper towel. He leaned heavily on the sink and took a deep breath.

Two years ago, he was on top of the world. A happy marriage, two lovely kids and a promising career with EFT Bank. He was destined for great things. Where did it all go wrong?

Bob dropped the crumpled paper towel into the garbage can and took a final look in the mirror. He straightened his tie and smoothed his shirt, but there was no hiding the bags under his eyes. With a sigh, he headed back to his office, sat behind his desk and called his secretary. "Carol, I'm ready now. Please send Mr. Chapo in."

Bob straightened his tie again, cleared his throat and attempted to look comfortable. His clenched hands gave him away. A moment later, the door opened and his secretary showed a man into his office. Bob stood up to shake Chapo's hand, but the man was looking around the office and ignored his greeting. Bob let his arm fall to his side and hoped no one in the office was wondering about the guy in the baggy jeans, hoodie and cowboy boots with thick gold chains around his neck. And why he was there. He motioned Carol to close the door when she left.

Chapo finally took a seat on the other side of his desk and leaned back in his chair like he owned the place. "Mr. Stuart, I'm here to give you a message from our mutual client. Find a new bank and quickly. If what you say is true, there isn't a lot of time."

Bob stared at him for a few moments. "I don't think you understand. As I've told them, it'll take months to find another bank and"—he leaned forward and lowered his voice—"there's no guarantee another bank will want the accounts."

Chapo's smile creased his deeply pockmarked face. He threw one boot up on the desk, and Bob dropped back farther into his chair. "My clients understand perfectly well. And they want me to make sure you do too."

Was this a threat? Two years ago, Bob would have put on the charm and said anything to appease a client. But that was two years ago. "I told them it doesn't work like that." He hated the whine in his voice. "I can't magically snap my fingers and another bank takes over all the accounts. This is going to take months." Bob couldn't help rubbing his palms with his fingertips. He was itching to open his bottom drawer for a little shot of scotch.

Chapo clearly didn't care. He took his time looking at the large signet ring on the index finger of his left hand. "Señor, I'm just telling you what my client wants." He stretched his fingers in front of him, so the light caught the jewel of the ring. Then he lifted his dark eyes and found Bob's. "It's up to you whether you do anything about it. But understand this, there will be consequences. There are always consequences."

Bob had to make him understand. He leaned in again, like they were conspirators. "Look, I'm already under suspicion at the bank. My every move is being watched. There are rumours of an investigation. Do you understand?"

Chapo dropped his foot to the ground and stood up. "I think the question, señor, is do you understand? Please let me make it very clear. Like you, I have a job to do. And like you, I follow orders. I suggest you do the same." He turned and let himself out of the office, not bothering to close the door behind him.

Bob sat there catching his breath. He pushed his chair back, pulled his bottom drawer open and found what he was looking for. He poured himself a double and downed it, then dropped his head into his hands. He didn't care if Carol came in and saw.

What would people think when it all came out? No one would understand, let alone forgive him. How could they? He looked up, glanced at the bottle and then looked away. He had to stay sharp. But the worries that had been haunting him for the last year flooded back. What would Jani say? Would she leave him?

He thought about what he'd tell her. How it had all started with the gambling in Hong Kong and then just got out of control. That made him think about the journal he'd kept from his time in Hong Kong.

He unlocked his middle drawer, pulled out the journal from its hiding place beneath a stack of files and opened it. It read like a confession. Why had he written it all down? Did he want someone to know the truth—why he'd done what he'd done?

Because of the good parts too, he reminded himself. Things he wanted to remember. Like when they'd arrived in Hong Kong and were met at the airport by a chauffeur in a Mercedes limousine. Their gorgeous apartment halfway up The Peak, with its 180-degree view of Victoria Harbour. The servants and nanny and pool—and no houses or apartments above them, only jungle. The holiday flats in Macau. The ocean-going junks they were free to use—eighty-foot-long boats that came with a crew and on-board cooking facilities. And the bank had paid for everything. Bob hadn't even paid income tax. He had never wanted to leave Hong Kong.

For a banker, Bob wasn't very good with money—something Jani had always worried about. When they lived in Vancouver, she'd wondered where the next penny was coming from, but in Hong Kong, even she was amazed at how cheap things were and how wealthy they'd suddenly become. Jani loved trips to the islands, especially the semi-annual visits to the Happy Valley racetrack where the bank bigwigs hosted Hong Kong's rich and famous. While Bob and Jani would put on twenty-dollar bets, he couldn't help noticing the locals would be betting thousands of Hong Kong dollars.

Gambling was very popular and not just at the racetrack. The nearby Macau casinos handled millions of dollars. Many of Bob's clients were big gamblers, and Bob was expected to join in. He knew little about gambling and was cautious at first. But he began to enjoy himself. And soon gambling became a regular part of his life.

As time went on, he knew going back to Vancouver would be difficult. While he was in Hong Kong, the bank's commercial business almost doubled. He was more successful there than he'd ever been. But Jani was looking forward to heading home. She missed her parents. And as she kept reminding him, the kids were getting older and the grandparents wouldn't be around forever.

Bob didn't want to leave. Didn't want to tell her about his gambling debts or that, although he'd been paid well in Hong Kong, he'd lost most of it. Returning home would be tough. Three years away, even from a city as small as Vancouver, might as well have been a lifetime. Then there was the cost of living. There'd be no allowance, no nanny, no complimentary transportation or membership at a fancy club—and worst of all, he'd have to pay income tax.

Bob closed his journal. Suddenly it didn't feel safe to have it here, even in a locked desk. What if his boss found it? Or the auditors? He tucked it into his briefcase. Then he stared at his empty whisky glass for a few minutes, wondering how long it would take the bank to figure it out. They'd been asking questions about his clients. Where did they get their money from, and what was the nature of their business interests? They said it was a new initiative to get to know clients, make banking more personal. But it didn't fool Bob. They were watching him. Doing more audits. Keeping an eye on wire transfers over a certain dollar amount.

The bank's senior credit officer had paid him a friendly visit, said he wanted to get to know Bob's clients better too. Bob was vague with his answers; claiming they were mostly referrals from clients he'd looked after during his time in Hong Kong. They were all good people, he said. But he knew the bank was going to dig deeper. It was only a matter of time.

Chapter 2

A week later, after several sleepless nights, Bob was late leaving the house. Jani had already left to drop the kids off at school.

When Bob stepped out of his front door, he stopped suddenly. Standing across the street was Chapo. Towering over him was a big fat guy that reminded Bob of a debt collector. They were staring at him. The fat guy waved.

Bob hurried to his car. As he drove out onto the street he expected them to follow. But they didn't. Was it another warning? He knew that sooner or later the people he'd been banking with would take steps to cover their tracks.

He'd run out of time. He had to tell his wife. He had to warn her. He gripped the steering wheel and took a curve too fast. She'd never understand. He'd lose her. And the kids.

When he pulled into the parking lot at work, he turned off the car and let his head rest on the steering wheel. If he was in the garage at home, he could just leave the motor running. Go to sleep and never have to think about any of this again. He'd almost done it two days ago after Jani had gone to bed. But the thought of her finding him had turned his stomach. He couldn't do that to her. Not after she'd stayed in Hong Kong for three years, miserable but patient. Having no idea what he was up to.

He lifted his head from the wheel and stared through the dirty windshield at nothing. Maybe there was another way. He thought about his old friend Bolton. He'd know what to do.

...

Paul Bolton hadn't heard from Bob Stuart in months. So when he got the message that Bob wanted to meet him urgently, he was puzzled. He called him immediately.

"There's something I need to talk to you about," Bob told him. "Can we meet today?"

"We're in the middle of packing," Bolton said. "We're off to the island first thing in the morning. You remember, our annual trip to Parksville. But we can chat right now if you fancy."

"No, no. When you get back is fine."

"We'll be away at least a fortnight—"

"It's okay. It can wait."

Bolton ran a hand through his blond hair. He couldn't quite place it, but Bob was holding something back. "Listen, you'd say if it was something serious, yeah?"

"Of course. Have a good time with your family, Paul. We'll talk when you get back." Bob hung up.

Bolton put the phone down and sat at his desk. Bob had sounded distant. This wasn't the old Bob he knew. He wondered what the problem could be. They'd only talked once during Bob's three years in Hong Kong, but he could tell his friend had fallen in love with the place. His career was thriving, and Bolton had felt a twinge of envy at the time, hearing all about Bob's visits to Singapore, Malaysia and Thailand. Places Bolton would have loved to have shown his own family. Growing up in England, he hadn't seen much of the world, apart from a six-month work assignment in Oman.

They'd met a few times since Bob had returned to Vancouver. Bob was a changed man. At first Bolton thought he was just missing the good life and was sure he'd settle down. And he had. Many of his Hong Kong clients followed him to Vancouver, chasing the hot real estate market. But the next time he saw Bob, his old friend looked thinner, paler. There were dark rings under his eyes. And the old charm was missing.

Bolton wondered if it was the stress of work. He'd heard from some people at the bank that Bob hadn't taken long to start bringing in new business for the bank. Slowly he was becoming the golden boy again. Had he been headhunted by another bank? Or were there problems at home? Bolton knew Bob's wife hadn't wanted to stay overseas once his contract was up. Bob had tried to persuade her, but it didn't work. Had things come to a head? Were they getting a divorce? Bolton was jumping to conclusions and, as always, assumed the worse. He shook his head. It was probably nothing.

Chapter 3

The following Monday morning, Jani Stuart stayed to have a coffee with her girlfriends after her workout. When she got home a little after eleven, she was surprised to see her husband's car in the driveway. When she'd left that morning to drop the kids off at school, she was in two minds about waking him up. She knew he was tired and hadn't been sleeping, so she left him in bed. But she would have expected him to be up by now.

Lately he'd been having a lot of late nights at the office and hitting the bottle hard when he got home. Was it another one of his hangovers? As she headed up the walkway, she made a mental note to talk to him about it. She'd need to pick her moment; he was so irritable these days. It was just easier to ignore the problem.

She opened the front door, dropped the keys on the entrance table and set her sports bag down on the floor. She walked into his office at the back of the house, but there was no sign of him. She glanced at the whisky glass on his desk and frowned.

Jani picked up a laundry basket and headed up the stairs and into their bedroom. Bob was lying on the bed fully clothed, eyes closed. Clearly he'd woken up and gotten dressed. Had he already been drinking this morning? She dropped the basket onto the wood floor, but he didn't stir.

"Unbelievable. He's passed out," she muttered. She leaned in and called his name, but he didn't move. She was about to get a glass of cold water when she noticed the small medicine bottle on the floor. Was he sick? Or was this just a hangover remedy? She picked up the bottle. It was empty. His name was on the label, but she didn't recognize the prescription.

"Bob?" A note of worry tinged her voice.

She placed her hands on his shoulders and shook him, but there was no response. She couldn't hear or see him breathing but could smell alcohol.

The next twenty minutes passed in a flash. The ambulance siren, the loud banging on the door. The two policemen on the doorstep. The paramedic looking up, shaking his head, saying, "I'm very sorry, Mrs. Stuart."

The police officer had caught her when her legs gave out. He helped her to a nearby chair. The paramedic came over and waved smelling salts under her nose. The cop offered to call a family member or friend to come over and stay with her.

She didn't remember calling her parents but did recall one of the policemen checking the house. She overheard him say to his partner that there were no signs of forced entry, and it looked like an overdose.

She stared at their wedding picture on the wall across from their bed. It was an overdose. No one had done this to her husband. He had done it to himself.

Chapter 4

Paul Bolton was stretched out on the warm beach, a two-day old *Vancouver Sun* in front of him, when he learned what happened to his friend Bob Stuart. The paper called it suicide.

Bolton made some calls to people he knew at the bank. They were all shocked at the news and didn't know anything more than what was reported in the newspaper. He cut short his holiday, leaving his family on the island, and drove back to the mainland to visit Bob's wife.

…

When Bolton arrived at the Stuart home, he was let in by Jani's parents, who were there helping with the kids. Jani was lying on the couch, looking out of it, probably drugged up on sedatives. She opened her eyes when he knelt next to her.

"I still can't believe it," she said. "I keep thinking I'm going to wake up and find this is all a bad dream. That he didn't do this … didn't leave me and the kids like this."

"Jani, I don't know what to say … I'm so sorry. He rang me just last week and wanted to meet. I couldn't make it. We were meant to meet up when I got back from holiday."

"He wasn't happy, Paul." She looked up with tears in her eyes. "I knew it. I-I ignored it. He was so difficult to talk to these past months.

It was easier when he was away—" She covered her mouth with her hand, as though she couldn't believe what she'd just said.

Bolton reached out and placed a gentle hand on her shoulder. He didn't know what else to do. He'd seen the same change in Bob.

She wiped a tear, cleared her throat and took a few breaths. "He'd been making business trips to Hong Kong and Vegas. He was always worse when he got back. He lost touch with friends…"

"So you've no idea what he wanted to speak to me about, then?"

She shook her head. "I just know he was working too hard. But I'm not sure it was work related. There was something else…"

"What makes you say that?"

She shrugged. "Just a sense. I know he was getting pressure from the bank about some of his clients." Her voice cracked and she started to sob.

Bolton looked around helplessly until he spotted a box of Kleenex. As he handed her one, he couldn't help wondering what Bob had gotten himself into.

Chapter 5

That evening, after the kids were finally in bed, Jani poured herself a glass of white wine. Then she got started on a task she'd been dreading. She pushed open the creaky door that led to Bob's office and looked around. Nothing had changed. He could have been there five minutes earlier, sitting in the swivel chair, hunched over his big walnut desk. She'd seen him at it so many nights when she'd stopped by on her way to bed to give him a kiss goodnight. She reflected that she'd done that much less in these past six months. There was a barrier slowly rising between them in the time before his death.

Jani took a deep breath and stepped onto the blue rug that covered most of the dark wood floor. They'd picked the rug together not long after moving into the house. It was before the children were born. That was another lifetime.

She took a sip of chardonnay and shook off the memories. She set down her glass and became determined as she opened drawers and rifled through files. She had to find the life insurance policy. She found it rather quickly, a thin file marked "Insurance." The amount of the life insurance had been circled in red. Two million dollars.

She felt a momentary relief. Bob had taken care of them. Of course he had. She set the file aside and wondered what else she should look for. Anything related to banking. A moment later she came across a renewal form for a safety deposit box. She didn't even know they had one. She set that aside as well, as a reminder. She'd have to call the bank tomorrow. Oh, why hadn't she been more involved in their financial affairs? Bob had always taken care of all that.

She was still cursing herself when she came across a folder marked "Debt." She stared at it for a moment. But they didn't have any debt. They'd paid off the mortgage a few years ago. And the car too. And she was always so careful with the Visa. She and Bob had agreed that they'd always pay it off in full to avoid the ridiculous interest charges. This must be an old folder. Her hand hovered over it. Or perhaps she would just see "None!" when she opened it. Still she hesitated. There was something ominous about that word, *Debt.*

She opened the folder and started to read, her eyes scanning the first page slowly, then faster, as fast as she could, flipping page after page, her eyes blurring with the speed, or were those tears? Yes, she was crying as she read notice after notice, overdue bills—and warning letters from the bank about—what was this? Missing mortgage payments. Jani reread that one. It was dated last month. They had a mortgage. They owed over $100,000. And from what she could see, they hadn't paid anything on it in some time.

Jani dropped the letter from the bank and frantically flipped through every page in the file, doing math in her head, adding everything they—no *she*—owed. There were statements from different finance companies, names she'd never heard of. Over two hundred thousand dollars. And three different credit card statements. She recognized only one card. The one they'd shared for more than a decade. She was always so careful when she went grocery shopping. Always buying the bulk bag of potatoes to save a few dollars. Never buying anything out of season. She was breathing fast, the shock becoming fury. She added up the outstanding balance of the credit cards. Almost eighty thousand dollars. A heaviness was settling on her, like a comforter she'd pulled out of the washer when the spin cycle didn't work properly, and she had to drag it to the back deck and hang it in the sun to dry off. Yes, it was that kind of cold, an impossibly heavy load. No amount of sunshine would fix this. She dropped to the floor, letting the papers spill around her, and began to sob.

Chapter 6

The next day, when Jani contacted the insurance company, it was as if they were expecting her call. The agent was polite but professional and direct.

"Madam, the policy on your husband's life has certain exclusions. One of them is that in the event of a suicide, the policy is void. The coroner's report states that was the cause of death."

Jani didn't move. "So … I don't get the money?" It was little more than a whisper.

The insurance agent confirmed her statement. Jani held the phone away from her, stared at it, willing the man to change his answer. She had a million questions. What if it wasn't suicide? What if it was an accident. But she was clutching at straws. She hung up.

She'd lose the house. She might even be liable for Bob's personal debts. She didn't know. But she'd have to find out quickly. She called the bank and made an appointment.

The following morning she was sitting in the bank manager's office with a cup of tea. He'd been kind when he realized she had just learned of the debt. He'd seen this kind of thing before, and he was truly sorry for her. He took her to her husband's safety deposit box, the one thing he had kept up payments on, and waited while she opened it.

...

That afternoon, Jani sat wrapped in a comforter on the couch, sipping a cup of Earl Grey. She looked at the mysterious item she'd found in her husband's safety deposit box. A journal. She set her tea down on the table next to her and opened it. She stopped reading every five or six pages to take it all in. His handwriting was so bad she had to reread several passages to make sense of it all. It took her almost three hours to finish it. Some pages had just a few lines, others were filled. Over the last few months, the entries had become shorter but more frequent.

The last entry was dated less than a week before his death. She cringed as she read it.

> *What have I done? What's going to happen to Jani and the kids? I must tell her the truth.*

She closed the book and sat back. Her husband of eighteen years had been living a double life. Maybe suicide wasn't so unbelievable. After all, he'd had a gambling problem she hadn't known about. He'd even tried counselling without her knowing. And he'd gotten so deep into debt without even thinking of what he was doing to the family. She gripped the journal so tightly her hands ached. With a small scream, she threw it across the room.

"You selfish bastard!" The outburst didn't solve her problems, but it made her feel a little better.

She was furious at him for not confiding in her and yet felt guilty that he was never able to. She tried to think back. Of course she'd noticed a major mood change, but she'd been so busy raising the kids. And he'd been so prickly. Impossible to talk to. And she'd gotten used to his being the breadwinner, making sure she and the family never went short. She'd gotten lazy. Assuming everything was fine. That he was paying the bills.

She crawled over to the journal and picked it up. This book was the last piece of him she could hold. It had given her a window into his true being. A little voice niggled in the back of her mind. Yes, he'd gambled and gotten into debt. But there was more. Hints of illegal activities. Names of people she'd never heard of.

Had it all become too much, and the best way out was suicide?

She flipped the journal open to an entry dated a few days before he died: *I'm going to talk to Bolton. He'll know what to do.*

As she closed the journal, she wondered if he'd really chosen death over them. Surely the man she knew wouldn't have left her and the kids like that.

Jani stood up and carried the journal to the phone in the kitchen. She dialled Bolton's work number and told him about the journal.

"What's in it?"

"I-I'd rather you read it yourself. It's—well, he was involved in something, Paul. I think it's what he wanted to talk to you about."

…

Bolton wasn't sure what to expect when he arrived at Jani's house, and he was uncomfortable reading his old friend's private journal, worried about what he might find out. But he was also intrigued. What had Bob wanted to tell him?

Jani left him in the office, and he took his time going through the journal. He found himself going back over earlier pages, then skimming ahead to the time they'd moved back to Vancouver.

When he finished the journal, he sat back and thought of his old friend. He'd been caught in a trap. Bolton wondered when he'd reached the point of no return. He felt guilty that he wasn't there when his friend needed him most. If only Bob had told him how serious it was.

Bolton walked into the kitchen where Jani was sitting at the table. She looked up and started to cry. Bolton walked over to her and patted her arm gently. He'd never been comfortable with this sort of thing.

"Jani, I'm so sorry. I wish I'd known…"

"I lived with him for eighteen years and I had no idea. All those secrets for all that time. I tried and tried to get him to share his problems. But this. I never expected this. Not in all my worst nightmares. What should I do?"

Bolton grit his teeth. *What Bob should have done weeks ago.* "Go to the police. It sounds like he was frightened. Like someone was threatening him." He glanced down at the journal. "This might explain how he died."

Jani was quiet for a moment. "That occurred to me," she said softly, "that it might not have been … suicide."

Bolton stepped back and nodded. "It doesn't give us exact details, but…" Bolton sighed. "I'm sorry, Jani. It just seems like Bob was mixed up in something … dodgy. His debts, the pressure he was under…"

Jani nodded. She didn't want to hear this, but was it worse than the alternative? "I'd like to believe he wouldn't take his own life and that he didn't leave us on purpose." She wiped her face with a Kleenex. "But is it dangerous? I mean for me and the kids … if I take this to the police?"

Bolton wasn't sure. But his gut told him there was no reason these people Bob owed money to would go after Jani and the kids. "Can I take the journal? I know a police officer."

Jani agreed. She was relieved her husband's old friend was helping. And she wasn't sure she wanted to see that journal again. Even though it had some happy memories in it.

Bolton pulled on his coat. Before she closed the front door behind him, he turned back to her. "And Jani, don't tell anyone about the journal."

Chapter 7

Over the next few days, Bolton left messages for his old friend Pat Lossan at the RCMP Commercial Crime Division in Vancouver. He finally caught him in the office and explained what had happened. Lossan told him to come over and bring the journal.

Bolton hadn't seen Lossan in nearly six years and wondered how he was doing. He'd heard that he'd turned down a promotion to Alberta. His wife wanted their kids to graduate high school before another move. He knew Lossan put family first and had resigned himself to staying in Vancouver until the kids went off to college. He'd spoken to him a few times, but they never seemed to meet up for that beer they'd been talking about.

When Bolton arrived at Lossan's office on Heather Street, Lossan greeted him with a broad smile and bright eyes that lit up the room. He gave Bolton a big bear hug. As they settled into their chairs, Bolton noticed that his old friend had put on a lot of weight. He'd always been a big guy, but muscle had turned to fat, he had a double chin, and his belt was struggling to keep his stomach in. Lossan always had a sweet tooth, and his wife was a fantastic cook.

Lossan listened patiently as Bolton walked him through the journal, then took a moment to reflect on what he'd just heard. "The journal isn't evidence of a crime," he said.

"Maybe not. But there's something dodgy going on, Pat. I know he was a bit low, but I really can't believe he'd take his own life. And he rang me out of the blue a few days before he died. There was clearly something on his mind. Said he wanted to meet. I couldn't make it … and now he's dead. I don't know what's going on, but my gut tells me this is more than just gambling debts."

"What does the autopsy show?"

Bolton sighed. "Alcohol in his system. And sleeping pills— enough to kill three men."

"No sign of foul play? No break-in at the house?"

"I know how it looks. But no matter how bad things got, he'd never have abandoned his family like that."

"Maybe he was more depressed that you realize—"

"Yeah, but what about the names in the journal? He mentions a bloke called Alarez, and it sounds like he's tied to organized crime. And some of these new clients he's brought in since returning to Vancouver? Doesn't sound exactly above board. Like he didn't want to deal with them but had no choice. What if this is bigger than just Bob? What if his bank's caught up in something dodgy?"

Lossan shook his head. "Slow down. We don't know anything yet—except that your friend had some serious gambling debts, and from the sounds of it, he borrowed a lot of money and was under pressure to pay it back."

"I'm just saying, its worth having a proper look at the journal. I knew Bob. He's not the type to take his own life. Not a chance."

Lossan sat back and scratched under his chin thoughtfully. It was a familiar action that would have made Bolton smile if he wasn't so upset.

"Who really knows what goes through someone's mind when they're thinking of suicide," Lossan said. Then he looked at Bolton. "Let me read the journal and I'll tell you what I think. What are you going to do in the meantime?"

"I'm going to ring his boss at the bank," Bolton told him. "See what he makes of the journal."

"You sure that's wise?"

"So you reckon there might actually be something in this after all?"

"I'm just telling you to be careful. If Bob's boss was involved, he won't take kindly to you investigating his affairs."

Bolton stood up and looked out the window, then turned to Lossan. "Something's not right, and if no one steps up, this will all be swept under the rug, along with Bob."

Lossan sighed. "Always playing the Boy Scout. Listen, just let me do some digging. I'll read the journal, check things out and get back to you. Don't do anything until you hear from me. If your crazy imagination is correct, there may be someone inside the bank that's part of it."

...

When he got to work, Bolton tried to put Bob and the journal out of his mind. He wanted to follow Lossan's advice, but he couldn't stop thinking about things. He convinced himself it couldn't hurt to just talk to Bob's boss at the bank, a guy named Ed Landy.

"Bugger it," Bolton muttered, and he picked up the phone. A few moments later, he had Landy on the line. He told him bluntly that Bob's wife had asked him to find out what really happened to her husband.

There was a long moment of silence on the other end of the line while Landy seemed to be considering what Bolton had said. "She doesn't believe it was suicide?"

"She doesn't know what to think. She just can't believe he would end his life."

"Well, of course. That's never easy for anyone to think about." Landy sounded more animated now.

"Jani reckons it had something to do with work." Bolton hesitated. He wasn't sure if he should tell Landy about the journal. But Bob's journal made no reference to the man, so there was a good chance Landy didn't know a thing about what Bob had been up to. "Seems she found a journal Bob kept. It mentions … well, some things going on at work. Things might not have been entirely above board."

Bolton could hear Landy take a deep breath. "What kinds of things?"

"I don't know all the details … it doesn't matter … I-I'm just asking if you know…" Oh bloody hell. What was he supposed to say? *I'm just wondering if you were helping my friend Bob do something illegal at the bank.* Bolton cleared his throat.

"Who else knows about this journal?" Landy asked.

"You're the only person I've told," Bolton lied. "And Jani hasn't said a word to anyone else. She didn't even read it. Just handed it over to me." He didn't know if that sounded believable, but it occurred to him that this could get Jani in trouble too.

There was a long pause. Landy seemed to be weighing his options. Bolton knew he wouldn't be able to resist finding out about the journal. Even if he wasn't involved in any shady business, he'd be curious. A moment later Landy said, "Listen, I'm happy to meet and give you a bit of background, but not here at the bank. Let's meet somewhere private."

. . .

Two hours later, Bolton met Landy in a downtown bar on Georgia Street. The place was crowded but Bolton managed to get a table in the corner near the front window. On his way to his seat, he left his name at the host station and asked them to direct Landy to his table. After waiting ten minutes, he ordered a ginger ale. Five minutes later, his nerves were starting to show. He wished he hadn't chosen something with so much sugar. He was beginning to regret his decision to contact Landy. He should have listened to Lossan. *Just relax,* he thought. *It's natural to be concerned for a friend.*

"Did you bring the journal?" Landy asked, startling Bolton, who looked up at the banker.

"No. It's in a safety deposit box." Bolton wasn't sure how much he was going to share with Landy. For now, he just needed to get a sense of the man.

Landy smiled and sat down. "Listen, why don't you drop it off with me at the bank and I'll make sure it gets into the right hands. The bank will want to deal with this internally. I recommend you don't discuss this matter with anyone else."

Bolton smiled back, cleared his throat and pushed his glass away from him. He was stalling, figuring out how to respond. Landy seemed eager to get his hands on the journal. Bolton was never good at bluffing. He didn't even have a plan.

"I'm wondering," Bolton began slowly, "if you noticed anything out of the ordinary about Bob since he got back to Vancouver."

Landy stared at him for a few moments, probably wondering what he should say. "When Bob came back from Asia, he took a while to adjust," Landy said finally. "He missed Hong Kong, and coming back was tough on him. He had to prove himself all over again. As time went on he started putting deals together. Mostly new business with old clients from his Hong Kong days. In no time he was the golden boy, couldn't do anything wrong."

"So what happened?"

Landy leaned across the table. "Listen, and remember, you haven't heard this from me, right?"

Bolton nodded.

"All of Bob's accounts were solid, but questions were being asked."

"What sort of questions?"

Landy looked out the front window where people were streaming past and then looked at Bolton. "Who Bob's clients really were, and where their money was coming from."

Bolton was thinking fast. It didn't sound like Landy was involved. But he'd never been great at reading people. As his wife liked to say, he was an eternal optimist. What if Landy was just leading him down the wrong road? Getting information from him? He'd made a mistake. He should have listened to Lossan.

He looked out onto Georgia Street. It had started to rain, and he could see more umbrellas. *That's where I should be*, he thought. *Heading home.*

"I signed off on some of his accounts," Landy said, drawing Bolton's attention back to their table. "They were that large. I had some questions for Bob. He claimed they were all referrals from clients in Hong Kong. He said he knew these guys and vouched for them."

"So what was the problem?"

"Look, Bob didn't follow all the procedures for new clients. The bank was unhappy with some of his answers. There are strict disclosure requirements. Right now there's a witch hunt going on in the bank; they're trying to figure out what happened and who was involved. There's an outside investigation and they're looking into his clients."

"Just *his* clients?"

"Yes."

"So what happened?"

Landy opened his mouth and closed it again. "I've already told you too much. But if you want to give me the journal—I might be able to help."

"No," Bolton said flatly. Then immediately regretted his tone. He should have kept the guy talking, maybe promised to get it. But it was too late.

Landy stood up. "Bob and I go way back, and I'm sorry for his wife. But I-I can't help you." He turned around and headed for the door.

Bolton sat in the bar trying to take it all in. Talking to Landy had been a big mistake. He'd been hoping to shake something loose. All he'd done was stir things up. If Landy was involved, then now he knew Bob had kept a journal and Bolton had seen it. It meant that he and maybe even Jani could be in danger.

One thing was for sure. He had no intention of giving him the journal.

Chapter 8

Bolton couldn't sleep that night, and at two in the morning he headed downstairs to make himself a cup of tea. He kicked himself for contacting Landy and telling him about the journal. He should have called Lossan and told him what happened, but Lossan didn't seem to be taking the whole thing all that seriously.

His wife came downstairs as he was pouring the boiling water into his mug. "What's the matter, love?"

"It's all good. Just thinking about Bob." He set the kettle down distractedly. "I just can't believe what's happened."

Holly put her arms around his waist and leaned her head against his chest. "I can't imagine what his wife must be going through."

He nodded. What was he doing? He had a wife and three young kids. If Bob had been dealing with some crime gang, then Bolton's whole family could be at risk. He tightened his arms around his wife. *Let the police deal with it.*

But he knew he wouldn't leave it alone. He had to find out.

...

When Bolton contacted Landy a few days later, he discovered he was no longer with the bank. Without thinking, Bolton decided to leave work early and headed to Landy's house in North Vancouver. It was a relatively new neighbourhood, close to shopping and recreational facilities. Landy's house was like all the others in the neighbourhood: two-storey, nice lawn, double-car garage, well maintained. There were a few cars in people's driveways and the odd camper van. He passed two different landscaping company trucks on the street. Obviously a wealthy neighbourhood where people could afford gardeners. Landy must be in his late fifties. His kids, if he had any, would have left home.

Bolton parked on the road and walked up the driveway. The curtains were closed and there was no car in the driveway. After knocking loudly on the door several times, he walked over to a neighbour's house. A man in his mid-sixties answered the door. "He and his missus have gone south. Bit earlier than usual, but they go for a few weeks every year."

"You don't happen to know how to get hold of him?"

The man shook his head. "You might try three doors down. The Thomases are good friends. They may know how to reach him." Landy was gone. He thought about checking with the neighbours, but something told him it would be a mistake.

Bolton was going to tell him that he'd decided to share the journal with him after all and was just waiting for the banker's wife to get the journal back from the safety deposit box. But that wasn't true. The real reason for the visit was to get more out of him.

But Lossan had been right. He needed to stay out of it and let the cops handle things. He headed home to call Lossan.

...

Bolton's hands were shaking as he dialled Lossan's office number. But his friend wasn't there. Bolton told reception that he needed to speak to him right away, but he didn't hear from Lossan until almost ten o'clock that night.

"Sorry, Paul. It's been a busy day. Dispatch said it was important."

Bolton explained that he'd met up with Landy.

"You what? Why did you do that?"

"I know, I know. I just couldn't help myself."

"Listen, you can't go off doing this on your own."

"Well I didn't think you were taking it seriously ... and now Landy's disappeared."

"Slow down," Lossan said, getting into cop mode. "What do you mean, 'disappeared'?"

"I called the bank today. He's no longer with them. So I went to his house—"

"Listen, I know I joke about you being a Boy Scout, but you can't go snooping around. And you should not be bugging someone at home. You could get yourself into big trouble."

Bolton pressed the phone against his ear and closed his eyes for a moment. "I know you're right. But, Pat, his next-door neighbour reckons he's gone south, and they don't usually go south until the holidays."

Lossan sighed. "So he hasn't disappeared. He's just gone a few weeks earlier than usual."

"Yes. But why would he leave the bank?"

"That is an odd coincidence. I'll give you that."

Bolton relaxed a bit.

"Paul, I want you to know I'm taking this seriously. I've been in touch with CSIS. That guy Alarez from the journal, well, it turns out there's a Alarez right here in Vancouver who has connections to organized crime. If it's the same guy, maybe there's something to Bob's journal entries. My CSIS guy put me in touch with someone at the DEA." He paused. "So now maybe you won't go off on your own like the Lone Ranger?"

Bolton had been holding on to the hope that his friend had gambling problems and couldn't face up to what he'd done. But Alarez was real. Bob had somehow been connected to something very dark. Bolton couldn't believe what he was hearing.

"You still there?"

"Yes, sorry. I can't believe how foolish I've been." Bolton was thinking of his kids upstairs in bed and his wife watching television.

Lossan was going to tell his old friend that this was a police matter. But he also knew Bolton wouldn't stay out of something like this. Not when it involved a friend. And he was the best forensic accountant Lossan knew.

"Listen, the next step is to investigate the companies your friend was financing."

Currency exchanges and pay day loan operations, Bolton thought. *The types of businesses often used for laundering money.*

"See if we can figure out how they got their money out of Canada and back to Mexico… Are you still there?"

"Yes, I'm just trying to take it all in."

"If you want to be involved, you could help. But we need to move fast. The DEA suspect that, if the cartel is involved, they'll quickly shut down the businesses to avoid detection."

Bolton had forgotten how pumped up Lossan could get. He seemed to delight in going after the bad guys. Only Bolton wasn't sure he wanted to find out what really went on. Bob used to be such a good friend; it was hard to believe he was mixed up in all this.

Chapter 9

The following day, Bolton headed to South Cambie, a neighbourhood away from the bustle of downtown Vancouver, where the old Heather Street building that housed the RCMP offices had been built as a private boy's school before the First World War. Langara Academy hadn't lasted long and was converted to a miliary hospital for war veterans before the RCMP acquired it in 1920. Bolton hadn't been there in a long time.

When he got to Lossan's office, his friend had just gotten off the phone with the DEA offices in El Paso. The DEA agent had told him Bob's death could be the work of a cartel based in Sinaloa that ran cocaine, heroin and narcotics into BC.

"The Sinaloa cartel? Where does Bob fit into all this?" asked Bolton.

"They may have forced him to finance their so-called legitimate businesses and used his bank to clean the funds, then transferred them back to Mexico through the bank's US network."

"Forced him?"

Lossan raised an eyebrow. "There are plenty of ways." Both men were silent for a moment. Lossan reached across his desk and handed Bolton a thick file. "First things first," he said. "Read this."

Lossan found Bolton an office down the hall from him and showed him where the coffee machine was located. "Call me on extension 226 when you're finished."

Bolton read the DEA report slowly. He was taking it in and coming to terms with the fact that someone he'd known for decades was capable of things he couldn't imagine.

The first part of the report outlined some of what Lossan had already told him. The DEA had intercepted calls from the Sinaloa cartel to a Canadian number. One discussed payment to an operative. One was about moving twenty tons of marijuana up to the Canadian border. Others discussed deeds to properties in Vancouver and plans to buy a money exchange bureau.

When Bolton got to the second part of the report, he reread a few passages that discussed the man called Alarez, who was apparently the local cartel representative. The twenty-five-year-old Mexican was enrolled in a business course at Langara College, but according to the report, the real purpose of his move to Canada was to coordinate the cartel's drug operation. He'd been on the DEA's radar for a while. The college was less than twenty blocks from police headquarters.

Bolton got up and headed down the hall to stretch his legs and get a coffee. He'd often dreamed of getting involved in an investigation like this and had almost forgotten that it had cost his friend his life. He'd been taught to be careful what he wished for. But he was an opportunist and not the type to flinch from a curve ball. He saw life's twists and turns as opportunities. That was when real character shone through. Like the time he'd signed up to join the RAF Volunteer reserve to learn to fly, or the six months he'd spent in Oman while training to become an accountant. He never learned to fly, because he suffered from air sickness and migraines. Nor did his time in the Middle East turn out to be quite the adventure he'd expected. But both had helped shape his character and made him what he was today. Always trying new things, stretching himself and not always taking the easy path.

He returned to his desk, put his feet up on the chair opposite and leaned back with the report open to where he'd left off. After a few moments, he leaned forward, dropping his feet to the carpet, and opened the small notebook he'd brought with him. He began writing down some of the important points he'd gleaned from the report. He reread his notes.

> *Sinaloa cartel connected to Canadian crime gangs. Flooding the nation with drugs. Huge profits on cocaine shipments to Los Angeles, Chicago and New York. Vancouver now a base of operations. Offshore bank accounts used to hide the money. Size of the cash involved means cartel likely using a financial institution to transfer money south of the border and maybe overseas.*

This gave Bolton pause—could this have been what Bob was into? He didn't want to think about it, but it was impossible to avoid. He had to accept it. Bob Stuart had been banking a drug gang, and whether by suicide or murder, it led to his death.

Bolton set the report down and called Lossan. His friend appeared in the room a moment later.

"So where do we go from here?" Bolton asked.

"I'm going to meet with the DEA down in Texas. They know the Sinaloa cartel firsthand, how to proceed—and the risks involved."

Bolton stood up to leave. "Let me know what you find out."

Lossan laughed. "I was hoping you'd come with me."

Bolton didn't know what to say. He'd already exposed himself to Landy, who'd suddenly disappeared. Could he risk getting involved just to help his old friend's wife find out what happened to her husband? He'd talk to his wife and let her know what was going on. He wanted her to be okay with this. He also needed to tell her who they were dealing with. "I need to think about this. Can you give me a few days?"

But Lossan already knew the answer. He could see it in Bolton's eyes, the adrenalin kicking in. The Boy Scout could never resist a challenge.

Chapter 10

As their plane circled El Paso on a clear November morning, Bolton noticed the mountains in the distance. He'd read that even though they were only at 3,700 feet, the altitude combined with the dry desert air could cause altitude sickness. Maybe that was why he was feeling this way.

They were met at the airport by special agent Carlos Adriano. Adriano was a second-generation Mexican American. Bolton put the guy in his early forties. His tall frame, youthful looks and lean physique hid years of tough field experience.

Adriano's career had taken him from the Texas border to Puerto Rico, Turkey and Afghanistan's opium poppy fields. Now he was back in the DEA's divisional office in El Paso, which was responsible for West Texas, from El Paso to Midland, and all of New Mexico, an area that covered three hundred miles of the Mexican border and one of the busiest land crossings in the States.

About thirty minutes later, they arrived at a large modern-looking complex that housed both the DEA's El Paso office and the FBI. The giant compound was surrounded by tall chain-link fencing and security cameras. There was only one way in and one way out. As they stopped at the guarded entrance, they were asked to show identification. After clearing gate security, the agent drove on and parked his vehicle.

As Adriano got out of the truck, he told Bolton and Lossan to leave their suitcases in the trunk. "We'll spend an hour here and then grab lunch."

He led them through the main entrance, where everyone had to be scanned. There were two sniffer dogs, and they were made to open their briefcases. After clearing security, they followed Adriano into a big reception area and then past several offices occupied by agents. Some were sitting at their desk on the phone, some had their feet up and were reading reports. None of them batted an eye at the visitors.

Inside the main office, there was a forty-foot-long wall covered with charts and photos. Many of the images were of mutilated bodies. Bolton noticed some were children about the same age as his kids.

Adriano caught Bolton staring.

"Gruesome, I know. It's important to understand who you're dealing with. These cartels will do anything for money. Even murder their own brother or sister. Last year in Juarez there were eighteen hundred deaths. Drive into the interior and you'll see bodies left on the side of the road. They don't bury them. They're sending a message." Adriano looked at his guests and grimaced. "Maybe a short history lesson?"

Bolton felt like throwing up. Why was he involved in helping the cops track down the cartel? Finding out what happened to his old friend was one thing, but this was something else. Why was he exposing himself and his family to people that could do things like this. Murder meant nothing to them, even their own family, if it got in the way of business. Is that what happened to Landy? Had the cartel silenced him? And would he be next?

Lossan nodded. "By all means."

Adriano poured cups of coffee and handed a mug to each of them. "America has a huge appetite for narcotics. In the late nineteenth century, about three percent of the US population was supposedly addicted to morphine. A century later America was consuming up to seventy percent of the world's production of cocaine. In 1970, a CIA report estimated there were at least half a million heroin addicts in the US.

"By then over forty percent of US high schoolers were using marijuana. But you know what? In Mexico City, less than four percent of the kids smoked it even once. And there was virtually no evidence of heroin use in Mexico."

Bolton looked surprised. "So the US fuels the demand for drugs and Mexico's poverty makes it the ideal supplier."

Adriano nodded. "In Mexico you could earn as much growing a single marijuana plant or a window box full of poppies as you could driving a cab for a whole year."

Lossan knew life in Mexico was cheap, but this sounded hopeless. He figured even the cops would be on the take, and why not? Their little problem in Vancouver seemed like nothing compared to what was going on in Mexico.

"What steps have the Mexican authorities taken?" asked Lossan.

Adriano laughed. "Sadly, my friend, Mexican politicians look to harness the income from illegal drug trading. For a long time, politicians were paid to protect drug lords. Those who didn't pay were arrested." He shrugged. "Or even murdered. State agencies became Mexico's mafia. Then national institutions like the Mexican federal police took over the protection rackets.

"Corruption changed from a mechanism that greased the wheels and oiled the machine to what we call the 'grand corruption.' These new racketeers have no links with the communities they extort. With profits from drugs and a weakened police force, now the traffickers are in charge. They still pay the authorities, but they decide the rules."

Bolton kept looking at Lossan and wondered if he comprehended who they were dealing with. Lossan caught his eye and nodded, as if to say, *Jesus Christ, what have we let ourselves in for.*

"Unfortunately, corruption does not stop at the border," Adriano continued. "Profits from the drug trade are tough to resist. Many local sheriffs, even DEA and CIA agents, look the other way."

"But your country has spent a lot of time and money on anti-drug policies," Lossan said.

"That's for sure. But not all the policies make sense. And mostly they target kingpins, not the greased palms. If you dig into it, you'll see these policies are often driven by the need to raise cash or find a scapegoat. When someone gets arrested, it looks good for the government. It's a win. So they target whatever group is easiest to break, so they can sell it to the public as a victory."

Lossan was surprised. "You don't agree with your country's drug policies?"

"Too often our policies are created to win votes at the ballot box. And these small victories never make more than a dent in the problem. American drug demand is too large. And of course, along with all the addiction and death caused by the rise in trafficking"— Adriano swept his hand in the direction of the images of mutilated bodies—"comes a massive rise in violence."

Lossan nodded, wondering if the DEA agent had seen too much. Twenty years fighting drug trafficking must have made him cynical and bitter.

"And things have gotten even worse in recent years," Adriano continued. "Criminals demand protection money from everyone— car thieves, human traffickers, local businessmen, truck drivers, even farmers. The game is simple: pay up or we kill you."

Somewhere during Adriano's speech, Bolton had begun to look out the window, his mind split between what he was hearing and the beautiful panoramic view he was staring at.

The DEA agent watched Bolton admiring the mountains. He wondered if he knew how many dark days he'd seen and how many fellow agents he'd watched die in the field. He sat down again, looked at them. "Any questions?"

"How are the cartels able to set up in Canada?" Lossan asked. "And how do they get the money in and out of the country?"

"Cash is their lifeblood; the cartel needs a bank or some business that's able to transfer funds through bank wires. This can be a complicated process. They probably have someone on the inside."

Bolton and Lossan looked at each other. They were both thinking of Bob—and Landy.

Chapter 11

They stretched their legs while Adriano went for sandwiches. Bolton's eyes drifted back to the wall of charts and photos. To the mutilated bodies of four children. They looked about eight or nine but could have been older. They'd been shot through the head and their throats were slashed, their bodies left by the side of the road. Bolton wondered if this was a warning to their parents. The senseless random violence was barbaric. Who would do this to children?

He was startled when Lossan put a hand on his shoulder and steered him back to the table.

Adriano returned with the food, and they each grabbed a sandwich.

"A few years ago," he said, "we got involved in a major drug bust. A Chinese guy named Zhenli Ye Gon was living in a four-storey mansion in Mexico City. One of his neighbours was the Mexican president. This place had a swimming pool, sauna, wine bar, even an elevator. We found over two hundred million in US dollar bills, some stacked in piles three feet high. Seventeen million in pesos, hundreds of thousands of Euros, Hong Kong dollars, Canadian dollars, gold bullion, jewels and eight vehicles. And just in case of unwelcome visitors, the guy had a stash of firearms."

Lossan was worried about Bolton. He was miles away, probably trying to comprehend the types of people that Adriano dealt with every day.

Adriano noticed too. "Señor, I'm sorry, but this is the world we live in. Greed is a terrible thing. Do you want me to carry on? We can take a break."

"No," said Bolton, "please go on. I just didn't see any of this coming." He turned and looked at the photos on the wall. "I've got kids of my own, probably the same age as some of the kids in the photos."

The agent looked at Bolton then back at Lossan. "Well if you're sure. Where was I? Oh, yes. Ye Gon. He claimed his company was a pharma manufacturer. It happened to be Mexico's largest importer of pseudoephedrine and ephedrine; chemicals used to make common cold medications. Chemicals also used to manufacture meth." Adriano paused.

"Turns out he was supplying a cartel based in Juarez. He was also an important client of Bitale Bank. It has a branch in the Cayman Islands. We believe the Sinaloa cartel has close to a billion dollars in offshore accounts."

He sighed. "The cartels are always coming up with new ways to launder money. A currency exchange is very common. They deposit it in small stashes to avoid government disclosure requirements. There are wire transfer companies that transmit money from the US all over the world. A few years ago, we arranged for a hundred grand to be paid through a well-known wire transfer company to the cartel. We told the company to deposit it in small stashes to avoid Mexican government disclosure requirements. When our agents questioned the wire transfer, the company made no secret of the fact that they knew the money was drug money."

While Bolton had been listening to the DEA agent, he was figuring out what it all meant for them. What would happen when they started investigating the various companies that had been set up to launder drug money? Once the RCMP had access to the bank's files, if there was someone at the bank who was part of the cartel's operation, they'd warn the cartel. That was clearly a risk the RCMP had to take. Surely the cartel would have covered their tracks and made other banking arrangements.

The whole thing was hopeless. Why was he here? Why had he gotten involved? They were dealing with people that would stop at nothing.

Lossan looked over at Bolton. "What are you thinking?"

"I was just wondering how we go about investigating these companies without alerting the cartel."

"I don't think we need to worry about that," Lossan said. "Chances are they knew the moment Bob's bank started looking into things. This isn't going to force them to leave town. They'll just find another way to launder the money. I'm more interested in finding out about their connections in Vancouver. It's not just some twenty-five-year-old Mexican. There's someone else behind the scenes…"

"Do you reckon the cartel might take them out?" Bolton asked.

Lossan looked at the DEA agent. "What do you think, Adriano?"

"It depends on who they are. If it's a local, then they might get rid of them. Unless, of course, they are well positioned to start up again somewhere else, now that this bank has been exposed. If it's one of their own, who knows? I would try and figure out if there is anyone else at the bank involved. But don't just look at Vancouver. Consider the US and Mexico as well."

Lossan was beginning to understand the challenge facing them.

Chapter 12

"Okay, gentlemen, if there's nothing else, maybe we can go for that ride I promised. I think as we drive through Juarez, you'll appreciate what we're dealing with."

Ten minutes later, Adriano nodded to the agent as they were waved through the Mexican border crossing into Juarez.

"I make this trip a dozen times a week. El Paso is one of the safest cities in the US. It has a population of over eight hundred thousand people, mostly Hispanic." He glanced at Bolton in the rearview mirror. "Juarez is just five miles away, and it has the second highest murder rate in the world. It has a population of over a million and there are over a hundred murders a year."

Bolton stared out the window at the abandoned homes and buildings covered in graffiti. He saw few street signs and no police vehicles. In fact, there were few vehicles of any kind. A woman with small kids walking along the side of the road glanced up when Adriano swerved to avoid a pothole and then a stray dog.

Bolton wound down the window, then changed his mind and quickly closed it. The acrid smell was awful. He knew the city was polluted, but his nose was stinging and his eyes started to burn. It was early afternoon, but it could've been an hour before dusk. The whole sky was grey with smog. He saw the occasional woman with small kids walking along a side street and lots of stray dogs.

Apart from the noise of the occasional vehicle, there was an eerie silence. They drove down a side street and Bolton gripped his seat as they approached what appeared to be a dead end. But Adriano turned a corner and found the main road again. They crested a hill, and in the distance the landscape was an outline of abandoned buildings and piles of rubble where homes had been demolished. They drove past a stretch of old abandoned homes with makeshift tents and passed under several bridges that occasionally carried traffic or pedestrians.

Bolton wondered how many times vehicles had been attacked as they drove under a bridge. He kept picturing gangsters ambushing them. It wouldn't take much—a few vehicles, a wrong turn. He sat back and closed his eyes, which were still watering. He willed himself to be somewhere else. Anywhere else.

Adriano glanced away from the rearview mirror and adjusted his hands on the steering wheel. "The cartel violence has led to a mass exodus of people. Thousands of homes abandoned. Many businesses just shut down. Most of the violence in Juarez is due to warring cartels. You may not know this, but El Paso has a large military presence. The US Department of Defense task force and the DEA's domestic field division are based here. We have our own intelligence centre and joint task force, and of course, the Border Patrol. The army base has tanks, artillery, attack helicopters—"

"That's a lot of fire power," Lossan noted, looking more grim than impressed.

Bolton opened his eyes and caught the DEA agent looking at him in his rearview mirror. "This is one of the most closely guarded border crossings in the country. Juarez happens to be the northern terminus of Mexico's national railway and has a large international airport. From here they can get anywhere in the US. And quickly."

Bolton remembered that Adriano had worked in Afghanistan, Turkey and Puerto Rico—he'd seen drug violence destroy towns and even countries. So how was he able to carry on day after day? Bolton made a note to ask him that evening. He hoped the tour would soon be over and he'd be back in the safety of El Paso. He closed his eyes again and must have drifted off, because when he opened them, they were crossing the border back to the States.

...

That evening, they met Adriano for dinner in a private room of a small local restaurant. He assured them the place was safe and they wouldn't be overheard.

Bolton was silent for most of the evening. A lot had happened in the years since he'd helped Lossan investigate the gang that was running George Koehle's mortgage company. At the time he was unmarried, and everything seemed exciting. Looking back on it, he realized that he'd been responsible for putting his then-girlfriend, Terry, in danger.

He and Terry had drifted apart after that. They'd both become busy at work, and then Terry was offered a promotion back east. She said she'd stay if they got married. Bolton just hadn't been ready to settle down.

It had taken him time to meet someone else. He wasn't sure if it was a mixture of guilt that made him shy away from female company or the fact that he'd buried himself in work. He'd started playing tennis again, and while he didn't go to many parties, he was often invited over to friends for drinks and sometimes to watch a football game. Without really knowing it, he'd fallen for a woman hired in his department for the summer. They bumped into each other by accident a few months after she left the firm. Holly suggested they meet for coffee. After a while they were meeting up on a regular basis.

Holly was six years younger than him. She was born in Ireland, but her family had moved to BC when she was a baby. Her father was a church minister, and every six years or so the family moved. They started off in Powell River, then moved to North Vancouver, then Prince George, then Peachland. It wasn't the whirlwind romance that you read about but more of a slow, steady relationship.

They bought their first home together in North Burnaby. Being a church minister, her father wasn't impressed that one of his daughters was living in sin. But within a year they were married in a small church, with Holly's father officiating. Two years later their first child was born. Bolton continued to work hard and progress at the firm. He and Holly now had two boys and a girl.

It was only when he was approached by a salesman that he realized he needed life insurance. They had a mortgage and three young children. For the first time he worried about the work he did, and what would happen to his wife and kids if anything ever happened to him.

"Paul, are you still with us?"

Bolton looked up and saw everyone staring at him.

"Sorry, I was lost in my thoughts."

"No problem," said Lossan. "What do you think?"

"Err..."

"Adriano was explaining the risks. He thinks the cartel's not going to take kindly to any sort of investigation that exposes them."

"So you're saying they'd target the police?" Bolton asked.

"Yes, but not just the police," Adriano told them. "They have no problem targeting DEA agents or their families. They'll cover their tracks and eliminate anybody they see as a threat. They're not going to give up their foothold in Vancouver easily."

Bolton leaned forward uneasily. "I met with a banker recently who might be connected. I let it slip ... well perhaps I gave the impression that we're beginning to investigate things at his bank. A week later, he vanished. His neighbour mentioned he'd gone south for a few weeks. As for the bank, they say he's no longer employed there but wouldn't share further details."

"I take it you think this is more than just a coincidence?"

"Yes. What do you think?" Bolton asked.

He looked at Bolton and then at Lossan. "Gentlemen, I don't believe in coincidences. And neither should you."

Lossan nodded. He was starting to get the impression that neither he nor Bolton were safe. Even two thousand miles away.

As Adriano dropped them off at their hotel, Lossan thanked him for his help. "Remember if you're ever in Vancouver, look us up."

The agent smiled as he got back in his vehicle and waved goodbye.

...

Lossan and Bolton met for breakfast the following morning before heading out to the airport.

Lossan tried to put Bolton at ease. "We need to find Landy. Find out if he's prepared to help us."

"You think he's still alive?"

"Look, it's hard to believe the cartel have dealt with him. We don't know if he was involved, and even if he was, then maybe the cartel has just tried to get him out of the way while they reorganize. You're just assuming the worst."

Bolton shook his head. "You heard Adriano. He doesn't believe in coincidences. And neither do I. I got involved to help an old friend's wife. If the cartel is involved, anyone looking into his death and asking questions about his bank is at risk."

"I understand but—"

"I don't think you do. I didn't get any sleep last night and it wasn't just the tequila. The last few days have shown me that no one is safe. I'm not going to put my family in danger…"

Lossan nodded. "I would never ask you to, Paul. I just thought, well, you're good at what you do. You could help a lot, going through all these companies Stuart financed … but if you don't feel safe, of course…"

They were silent for a few moments. Bolton felt torn. Was he overreacting? Was there really any harm in getting involved?

"I would want to keep my involvement quiet," he said finally.

Lossan agreed. "And I have another idea," he said, looking thoughtful. "I think there's someone else who can help…"

Chapter 13

Pat Lossan hadn't spoken to Alan Davis in years and had no idea if he'd be interested in coming to Vancouver, let alone working with him again. He hoped that Davis had gotten bored with the quiet life of the small town in the Maritimes and was up for a challenge. He had nothing to lose.

His boss told him it was a stupid idea and had limited chance of success. Lossan argued that if they did nothing, the cartel would slip through their fingers. The RCMP had started their own investigation into EFT Bank, where Bob Stuart had worked, but they were getting nowhere. The bank was using every trick in the book to slow the process, including an army of lawyers. Getting access to the bank's files anytime soon was hopeless.

Lossan thought they had to go about things differently. They weren't getting anywhere trying to find out what had already happened, maybe there was a chance he could get on the inside, use an undercover agent to connect with the cartel and give them an attractive alternative to the bank, a new way to launder their cash. But he had to act fast.

Years ago Davis had taken on an undercover role for the Quebec RCMP in a trucking company that was involved in drug trafficking at the port of Montreal. The notorious drug gang had avoided prosecution for years. When Lossan had first heard about the plan from his counterparts in Montreal, he was amazed they believed the scheme could work. He was equally surprised that Davis had agreed to do it. Eighteen months later the two officers who managed the operation told him that not only was Davis a brilliant undercover operator, but he was largely responsible for breaking up the gang and their stranglehold on drug trafficking at the port.

Convincing the ex-gangster to get involved was another matter. He might be concerned about returning to a city where he used to be well known in the gangster community. And working with the cartel would mean connecting with the local gangs that would do the footwork for the cartel.

Lossan hadn't given a lot of thought to an actual plan. The only thing he was sure of was that the cartel would be looking for other places to park their cash now that EFT Bank was exposed. And even if Davis wasn't prepared to act, he'd be a good person to run the plan by and see if it made any sense. In fact, he was hoping Davis would listen to what was going on and pipe up with his own ideas. And maybe be excited enough to play more than just a backroom role.

Chapter 14

Lossan hadn't heard from Bolton in a few days. Had he lost interest? Had their visit to El Paso put him off entirely? Lossan left him a few messages, but Bolton hadn't responded.

On a rainy Monday, Lossan dropped by Bolton's downtown office unexpectedly. When Bolton met him, Lossan was all smiles and gave him a big hug. Bolton knew what the visit was about, but he just poured them both a coffee and waited to hear what Lossan had to say.

"I was remembering the old times, when we worked together. You remember that case with George Koehle. You and me against the bad guys."

Bolton sighed. "Pat, I've talked to Holly—"

Lossan sat up, his eyes wide. "Not a direct role, of course. Just reading reports, looking through financial documents."

Bolton almost laughed. "I'm sure there are plenty of other firms that you can bring on board. I just need to put some distance between myself and a drug cartel."

"So you're turning me down?"

Bolton shrugged.

"Well I'm sorry to hear that. Pity really, it'd be a chance to catch up with an old friend. He's agreed to look at the plan and let me know what he thinks. Anyway, if that's your final answer, then fair enough."

Lossan stood up and was about to leave.

"What are you on about, 'old friend'?"

"Oh, I thought I told you. Alan Davis has agreed to fly out and meet. He may even be part of the team."

"I don't believe you."

"Well it's true. He's not committed yet but said he'd listen to what we have to say."

"You reckon that's going to change my mind?"

"Well it was worth a shot. Anyway he'll be here tomorrow. Why don't you at least come and say hi. See what he thinks."

...

Alan Davis hadn't been back to Vancouver in years, but when Pat Lossan called offering a free trip, he didn't hesitate. After an early breakfast in the hotel restaurant, he took a cab to the RCMP headquarters on Heather Street. Lossan greeted him in the lobby with a big smile, and Davis felt for a moment like he'd gone back in time— except the young corporal he remembered wasn't so young anymore. He'd lost some hair and put on weight around the middle.

Lossan brought Davis up to a conference room and introduced him to his boss, Jack Holliday. They were just about to start discussing the case Lossan had told him about when there was a knock on the door and Paul Bolton walked in.

Davis was surprised. He stood up and greeted Bolton, shaking his hand with his strong grip and holding his gaze for an extra few seconds. Unlike Lossan, the accountant didn't look much different from the last time Davis had met with him. He still had his blond hair, but Davis noticed the start of bags under his eyes. He wondered if that was work or kids, or maybe both. Davis remembered the time when he'd discovered Bolton was the person George Koehle had called for help. At the last minute, Koehle had gotten cold feet and figured that Davis was going to kill him. The bean counter had come to his rescue.

At the time he thought the accountant was stupid, one of those do-gooders who didn't know when to leave things alone. A few years later, as he reflected on events from the safety of Miramichi, he realized that Bolton was just doing what he thought was right.

Bolton forgot when he'd last seen Davis. He was still in good shape, and apart from his shaved head and grey stubble, he hadn't changed much. Bolton remembered how the cops had tricked Davis into turning against his own gang and then arranged for witness protection in return for his testimony against the gang. He'd taken an instant dislike to the guy and believed everything the cops had made him out to be. A lifetime gangster who'd stop at nothing. He wondered how Davis had reconciled himself to a life of always looking over his shoulder, wondering when someone from his old gang would catch up with him.

According to Lossan, Davis was the major reason a Montreal-based drug trafficking gang had been brought down. He was curious to know why someone like Davis had risked his own life to help the police.

When they were settled again, Lossan cleared his throat. "We now believe the sudden death of Paul's friend, a banker named Bob Stuart, is suspicious," he said. "Paul showed me Stuart's journal, and from the sounds of things, there's a good chance it wasn't suicide. We've since been able to determine through the DEA in El Paso that Stuart may have been helping a drug cartel out of Sinaloa, Mexico, clean their Vancouver drug money."

Davis caught Bolton's eye. Bolton's old friend had gotten himself in deep with criminals. Davis smiled to himself. Who would have thought the straitlaced bean counter would be friends with a dirty banker?

"It's early days yet," Lossan continued, "but we've decided to go after the cartel here in Vancouver and find out if there's anyone at EFT Bank, where Stuart worked, that might be involved as well. Also, Stuart's immediate boss, a guy named Landy, has recently disappeared."

Davis leaned back in this chair. "You're wondering if it's connected?"

"I reckon it is," Bolton said.

"You're right," Davis said.

"It might be," Lossan agreed.

"And it might not be," Holliday said distinctly. "Conjecture gets us nowhere."

Bolton could see what Davis thought of that from the look on the ex-gangster's face.

Lossan cleared his throat. "The DEA believes the cartel has gone to ground now that the bank's investigating all the accounts Stuart was managing. That means the cartel will be looking for other ways to clean their money." He turned to Davis. "That could be where you come in. We need to offer them a new home for their drug money. We'll use our contacts in El Paso to leak to the cartel the names of business brokers with clients who need money to grow their business." He raised an eyebrow. "You want to be one of those clients?"

Davis collected his thoughts, then looked back at Holliday. "What does your intelligence tell you about the Chinese gangs and money laundering in Vancouver?"

"Chinese gangs?" Bolton said. "What do the Chinese—"

"The triads," Davis clarified. "Chinese organized crime. They've been around for centuries and have a foot on every continent."

"Well … sure, they're in the city, everyone knows that," Holliday said, sitting up a little straighter. "You think the cartel is in bed with the Chinese?"

Davis stared at him. Were they really this out of touch? "Old news," he said.

Lossan frowned at him, but Davis just continued. "Look, they need a new way to clean their money—but they're not just going to jump into bed with another banker, especially when they have connections with the triad already. By now, they'll have started to shift their bank business that way. That's what I'd do."

Holliday was paying attention. He rubbed a finger under his chin as he thought about this. "Mr. Davis may have a point. The cartel's not about to blow their network in Vancouver. They're going to be very careful. They'll use someone they know."

"But how is the triad doing it?" Lossan asked. "I mean, how do they launder the cartel's money if they're not using a bank?"

These guys take forever to get to the point, thought Davis. "Casinos. They're using casinos to clean the money."

Lossan shook his head. "Adriano, the DEA agent we met with, mentioned cartels using casinos in Las Vegas, but we're talking about millions of dollars, maybe more. And this is Vancouver, not Vegas. They need a bank to move that kind of cash."

Davis was already tired of the conversation. No wonder nothing got done. "Trust me. They're using the casinos right here in Vancouver." He looked at Holliday. "You must have some intel on what's going on. Why the hell don't you get in there and start shaking things up?"

Lossan had forgotten how blunt Davis was. Bolton hadn't. It was one of the things he'd remembered about Davis when they first met. He said what he meant—of course, there was a lot the ex-gangster didn't say too. That was what made people suspicious of him at times. But Bolton felt he had a good sense of the man despite his guarded nature. He remembered thinking about Davis years ago—how he'd had the chance to kill George Koehle but hadn't.

Holliday leaned back in his chair. He was impressed. Lossan's idea to bring in Davis was a good one. They needed someone from the outside, a fresh perspective. A criminal perspective. But they also needed more than rumours. And he'd been hearing these ones for some time now. What they needed was proof.

"Yes, we've heard similar stories. But we have no evidence, Mr. Davis. And that can make it hard to proceed."

Davis looked like he was going to interrupt, but Holliday held up a hand. "An investigation takes time, and it must be done correctly, or anything we learn may not be usable in court. We'll take your opinion under advisement. But we need more than that." He looked at Lossan. "I'll arrange a meeting in a few days. Some of the boys have been working this angle for some time. They'll have insight into the problem."

Davis frowned. At this rate, they wouldn't be arresting anyone for a long time.

Chapter 15

For the next two days, Holliday and Lossan were on the phone lining up meetings at the RCMP's high-security facility in Langley. Holliday contacted Valeriy Boyko, an RCMP superintendent and senior officer with Canada's serious and organized crime unit and explained their problem. Boyko agreed to set up some meetings with his special task force officers, but he wasn't sure how other cops might feel about working with an ex-con.

"My thinking exactly, sir," Lossan agreed when Boyko said as much. "That's why we think it best to not mention his background quite yet."

"Okay, Corporal. But I'm going to do my own research. Check the guy out."

After the call, Lossan asked his boss if Boyko could help or if he was just another politician minding a desk.

"Pat, this guy's the real deal," Holliday said. "In his thirty years on the force, he's seen it all. Money laundering, drug trafficking, cartels, transnational crime syndicates, criminal intelligence, covert money operations and even terrorist negotiation."

Lossan wasn't convinced. He knew the guy wasn't much older than he was, and Lossan was still a corporal. Guys who got to this level were usually brown-nosers. He must have had friends in high places and knew when not to rock the boat. He needed to check him out.

...

A few nights later, Lossan met with an old buddy who'd left the force after fifteen years and gone private. Some big multinational security company, providing intelligence, anti-money laundering protection and corporate investigations. He'd been surprised but happy to hear from Lossan after all these years and had agreed to meet him in a bar downtown.

Lossan came straight to the point and asked Smith what he knew about Boyko.

"I've heard of him," Smith said. "Never worked with him. But I know he's well thought of."

Lossan set his drink on the bar. "Why's that?"

"Our company offered him a job. Big package making three times as much as he'd be making, plus a big bonus."

"So what happened?"

"Not sure at the end of the day. I gather he had some other commitments, something he wanted to finish. I guess the timing wasn't right."

"So is he as good as they say he is?" Lossan asked.

"I can check if you like. From what I remember he's had lots of joint projects with the US, Mexico, even South Africa." He took a sip of his bourbon. "The guy likes his overseas postings, war zones, hostage negotiation, that sort of stuff. That's why he'd have been a good fit. Apparently he has no time for politics. Something about interference of foreign governments in politics and law enforcement. Our guys didn't think he'd make it to pension, said he didn't always do what he was told."

"Oh yeah?"

Smith nodded. "Canadian politicians interfere way more with their police services than they do in the States, if you can believe it. I guess this Boyko calls it the way he sees it. Somewhere along the line, his card was marked."

...

A day later Lossan sat down with Davis and explained what they were doing.

"Sounds like a drug trafficking 101 course." Davis yawned.

"I'd forgotten what a smart ass you are," Lossan said. "Listen you've been gone from Vancouver for a long time, a lot has changed. Some of the guys we're about to meet could be very helpful. So maybe lose the attitude."

Davis smiled. "Do they know my history?"

"Not yet."

"These guys aren't gonna work with me and you know it."

"We'll soon find out."

Chapter 16

Doug Waddington wasn't sure about attending the meeting at Langley. If the British Columbia Lottery Corporation found out that he'd met with the cops on his own, he'd be out of a job. On the other hand, Waddington, who had been the corporation's anti-money laundering director for over a year, had received little support from his superiors. He was getting tired of the same problems and no solutions.

About a month earlier, Waddington had organized a summit for leaders in BC's casino industry to convince his bosses that the problem he was bringing to them was urgent. He brought in experts from the RCMP, casino regulators, bankers, and investigators from the Canada Revenue Agency and the Canada Border Services Agency to discuss the issue of money laundering in Vancouver casinos.

That's where Waddington had met Valeriy Boyko. And he soon discovered that Boyko's view of the world didn't always mesh with his superiors. Some viewed him as too aggressive and blunt. But he was known as someone who would take the most challenging files without worrying about the political consequences. As the senior investigator for the Canadian Revenue Agency in Ottawa had told him, "I don't care what you say about the guy, no one's taking more drugs off the street in British Columbia than Boyko."

Waddington had dealt with the triads back in Australia for years. The Chinese gangsters used complex business structures to hide their money and had an incredible ability to slip into society and spread their poison, like frost covers new shoots in early spring, turning everything beneath black. Their surreptitious nature made it challenging for law enforcement agencies to crack down on them. Waddington wanted to see how Vancouver authorities would handle things. He hoped that hearing from so many experts would convince his bosses to take the problem seriously.

And though everyone at that meeting had agreed funds were pouring in from China, there was disagreement regarding how the money was getting into the country. Capital export restrictions were supposed to protect the market from just this sort of thing. So how were the Chinese gangs getting around this?

Waddington had been disappointed with the summit. They'd accomplished little. And his bosses weren't any closer to changing their ways. The only way that would happen was if someone forced them to. It was as if they didn't care about what was going on in their own backyard.

But the truth was, senior management at the lottery corporation had revenue targets to meet. Their compensation was based on meeting those targets. And, of course, the government relied on those tax revenues from the gaming industry. So absent some public scandal, going after money laundering within the casino industry wasn't high on most people's priority list, and certainly not the people responsible for overseeing the industry.

Waddington knew that if you put up with things long enough without doing anything about it, you become part of the problem. He'd started thinking about going back to Australia. He'd enjoyed working there as a detective. That was when Boyko contacted him and asked if he could attend a private meeting with some of his people at police headquarters.

Waddington felt he had nothing to lose by going to the meeting. Maybe Boyko decided that it was time that the RCMP did something about the problem.

They met up at the force's high-security facility in Langley. Walking to the massive white complex from the parking lot,

Waddington felt his gut tighten. He turned in his driver's licence at the security desk behind a large glass wall, which he figured was bulletproof. The officer handed him a visitor's pass, and he was led through a turnstile and escorted into a conference room.

The billion-dollar federal building was the force's ultra-secure command and control centre where leaders would retreat and run BC in the event of a major disaster or terrorist attack. It was also a real-time intelligence centre where analysts monitored all manner of electronic records and signals.

Boyko and Waddington settled in the boardroom and waited. After a few minutes there was a loud knock on the door. Three tall guys walked in. Boyko stood up and introduced Waddington to Corporal Pat Lossan. Waddington had dealt with the RCMP on several occasions, but it was always in the presence of casino management, and he'd always been told to be careful what he said. He extended his hand toward the massive corporal and received a hearty handshake and a smile.

"And this is Paul Bolton, a forensic accountant," Boyko said, before motioning to the third fellow. "And this is Davis."

Just "Davis." Waddington was intrigued.

Boyko knew that Waddington would be uncomfortable attending the meeting. The more open he was, the more information Waddington might share. He needed to take Waddington into his confidence. He suggested they all take a walk to the operations room. As they headed over, Waddington couldn't help glancing at the newcomers. Lossan was animatedly chatting with Boyko. Bolton appeared more reserved but was in step with Lossan. Davis was trailing a bit, looking around quietly with intelligent eyes. The guy looked nothing like most cops he'd met. He was tall enough, but there was something about him that gave Waddington the sense he'd been on the other side of the fence. Perhaps it was the small scar above his eye, the jeans and leather jacket, the confident air as if nothing surprised him. Maybe Davis was an undercover cop.

The operations room had maps all over the walls, along with photos of suspects linked to other suspects and to businesses across

Richmond and Vancouver, all connected with coloured pins and threads. There were names of police investigations, lists of transactions, link charts, flow charts and hierarchy charts. The Chinese triads were clearly a focal point. Waddington felt as if he was a cop back in Melbourne sitting in on some big investigation. Boyko had taken him into his confidence. Any doubts he'd had about attending the meeting disappeared.

After the tour they returned to the boardroom. Boyko announced he had a few calls to make and would rejoin them later. They settled in with coffees, and Waddington looked up to see Pat Lossan smiling at him. His naturally friendly demeanour was hard to resist. Waddington relaxed in his chair as Lossan explained that they were exploring the possibility of money laundering in the Vancouver casino industry.

Waddington looked around the room. "Exploring? You mean you don't know for sure?"

Lossan didn't respond. Sometimes he pretended to know a lot less than he let on. He found it helped when he wanted a witness to tell their story. Interrupting them was often a mistake. He didn't care what they thought of him.

Davis looked bored. As if he already knew the answer.

Bolton just sat there with his pencil in his hand.

Waddington sat back in his chair. He assumed they had limited or no knowledge of what was going on in their own backyard. "Let me start at the beginning. First, how well do you know Vancouver?"

"I've lived here all my life," said Lossan. "Bolton's been here over twenty years, and Davis is from back east, he just got … posted here."

Waddington thought there was more to it, but he only said, "I used to be a cop in Melbourne. Gangs, money laundering, fraud. Couldn't turn down the chance to come to Vancouver. Director of anti-money laundering seemed right up my alley. Now I've been in this job a little over a year and it's almost as if I'm back in Oz, still acting like a bloody cop." He rested a meaty hand on his ample belly. In the short time he'd been working for the lottery corporation, he'd stopped most of his regular exercise and had a lot of late nights eating fast food. "Back home we had a large influx of foreign money. But things started to change, crime shot up, and there was a big increase in absentee property owners." He shook his head. "This is just like Melbourne a few years back."

Bolton wrote something down in his notebook. Davis and Lossan kept his gaze.

Waddington took a bite of a chocolate donut, then set it on the table. He felt as if he was being interviewed for a job. Lossan was the friendly smile, Bolton the note taker, and Davis the brains.

"I'm sure you're aware that Chinese money has been flooding into cities around the world." Waddington took a sip of coffee. "And Vancouver's an obvious choice to park a lot of their cash."

"Why?" Bolton asked, looking up from his notebook.

"Well for starters," Waddington said, "Vancouver's on the west coast, close to the US border and just a hop across the Pacific from China. And then there's your booming real estate market. Ever since Expo, the city's seen growth. And that's attracted international attention. The triads wasted no time figuring out how to launder drug money through property investments."

"How do you mean?" Bolton asked.

Waddington almost smiled. The accountant looked so sincere. He seemed to have little understanding of the complex organized crime pervasive in his city. Or was the accountant playing a role too?

Bolton bristled a little at the look he got from Waddington. "I mean I'm aware of laundering through financial institutions, of course..." He wanted to add, *Bloody hell, I'm not a kid.*

This made Davis smile.

"Well that's where the casinos come in," Waddington explained. "We've seen gamblers bring in suitcases on wheels, full of cash, and hockey bags stuffed with twenty-dollar bills ... some even carry cash in a plain brown lunch bag. They don't bother to hide it. At the River Rock our agents see bricks of cash wrapped in elastic bands shoved across the counter to the cashiers. The bills get tallied, and the cashiers exchange them for high-value betting chips. Then these guys play for a bit, lose a little and cash out. They wash the money in broad daylight. It's that simple." Waddington took a long sip of coffee and set his cup down. "Once the money's laundered, it's invested in expensive Vancouver real estate. Drives the market up and makes them even more money."

"How much are we talking?" asked Lossan.

"Hundreds of millions of dollars and as far as I can tell. It's been going on for a few years and increasing every year." Waddington let that sink in.

Davis leaned back in his chair. He was wondering how the triads managed to get their hands on that much Canadian currency. It wasn't coming from the Canadian banks.

"As I'm sure you know, there are restrictions on exporting currency," Waddington said. He looked at Davis as though he could read his mind. "So you're probably wondering how the money is coming into the country. Well I'll tell you how. The triads have established an underground banking network." He saw their blank faces. "You know about this?"

Lossan and Bolton both nodded. Davis looked over at them, thinking, *Liars. The buggers know fuck all about it, and neither do I.*

Waddington pretended not to notice. "Reckon Boyko's been investigating these underground banks for some time now. He suspected they're linked to the cartels, the Chinese triads and Vancouver casinos."

Lossan's ears pricked up at the mention of cartels.

"After lots of surveillance and investigations, they figured out how they're doing it."

Davis leaned forward, and Waddington couldn't help grinning at him. He was enjoying the reveal. "It starts when local loan sharks recruit whales—you know the high-roller types who lose a lot of money? The whales fly over from China and place orders for cash deliveries from the loan shark's company. The company loads up the cash in vehicles and drives it to parking lots near the casino. That's how these whales get the hockey bags full of cash to gamble with."

Waddington could tell that he'd finally told Davis something he didn't know. Lossan and Bolton on the other hand looked like Boy

Scouts who'd just been told they were roasting hot dogs stolen from the old lady down the road.

Waddington took a sip of coffee before continuing. He expected questions but there were none. He wondered how much they were taking in. They'd probably have Davis explain it all to them when he'd gone.

"Don't casino workers notice what's going on?" Bolton asked finally.

Waddington nodded. "One of my Sheilas who oversees the dealers told me the baccarat pit was getting out of hand, but management was ignoring staff's warnings. Most of the staff knows gangs are in the casinos—customers come in with black eyes, some of the high rollers conceal guns. And recently a VIP gangster publicly threatened to kill one of the dealers."

Lossan raised his eyebrows. "Why don't they report it?"

Waddington shrugged. "Everyone's intimidated. And it's just easier to ignore it. Play nice. Someone remembered seeing one of these whales shake hands with senior staff. They seemed to know each other well." Waddington loosened his tie and shifted in his chair. "So there you have it. The triads target Vancouver because it's easy and very lucrative."

"But what about you?" Lossan said. "The lottery corporation, that is. It seems you have all the information—"

Waddington dropped his mug onto the table and looked disgruntled. "Well it's just not that easy now, is it? I've been talking to my bosses almost since I started about what we're seeing. Whenever I kick a major investigation upstairs, it gets push-back. And the reason is simple: your politicians are afraid of losing the revenue. Oz wasn't any different. They were afraid to piss off the whales, worried that the tax revenue would go elsewhere. There's little incentive for government to change its ways. Do you know how much revenue these whales bring to casinos? And do you know how much of that falls into government coffers?"

Davis looked at Lossan. The big Mountie wasn't happy.

"But the good news," Waddington added, "is that slowly we're gathering information. We now know that one of the loan sharks running an underground bank also happens to work at the River Rock Casino, and he's funded by a business located in a Richmond office tower. The place happens to be down the road from the River Rock." He opened his hands upward in a gesture of incredulity. "It's a criminal bank operating in broad daylight."

Lossan grimaced.

"Oh, don't look like that," Waddington said genially. "You're on the right track now. I can tell you a few places to start. For one, check out the River District development on Marine Drive. The place is full of condo projects stacked up on the south side running along by the river. It's mind-blowing. Small units, high prices, all financed by offshore money and sold to offshore investors."

Bolton was making frantic notes, and Davis couldn't help wondering why he didn't use a laptop.

"Then there's Metrotown," Waddington said. "Like Richmond, it's thick with underground casinos. They're usually hidden behind currency exchanges or in the back rooms of karaoke lounges. The locations change weekly—oh, and when you check out the casinos, watch your backs. They have contacts inside the police. They'll know you're coming if you tell the wrong people."

Davis had wondered about that. His distrust of cops knew no bounds, though he doubted Lossan had given it a second thought.

The boardroom door opened, and Boyko walked in. "Sorry to rush you," he said to Waddington. "I'm afraid there's a few more people these guys need to meet. Corporal Lossan knows where to find you if he needs to follow up."

Lossan looked at Waddington and then Boyko. "Would it help if we had him stay and join us in some of these meetings?"

Boyko hesitated. Davis stood up and signalled to Lossan that he wanted a quiet word outside the room. Lossan was confused but followed Davis out.

"Listen," said Davis, "I don't think this is a good idea. We need to protect Waddington. He says he's under suspicion at the lottery corporation. Don't you think it's likely those guys have a cop or two in their back pocket?"

"Are you suggesting one of Boyko's guys is crooked?"

"Who knows? I just think we go slow, soak up all the intel we can, but don't assume all the cops are good guys. At this point, the less they know, the better."

"If we can't trust Boyko's own people who can we trust?"

"I'm just saying Waddington could be useful, we shouldn't put him at any more risk."

Lossan's body language told Davis he didn't agree with him. But clearly it was something he hadn't thought of.

They both returned to the boardroom. "Sorry guys," said Lossan as he looked at Waddington, "my associate is worried about exposing you to too many people."

Boyko was offended at the inference, but Waddington smiled. "Look, the less people that know about my visit, the better. I'm happy to help if I can, but time is short. Call me paranoid, but I might as well be an undercover cop."

Boyko reluctantly agreed not to mention Waddington to anyone else, then escorted him to reception where he exchanged his visitors pass for his driver's licence.

As he left the building, Waddington wondered what these guys were up to. Davis was clearly undercover. He didn't say much but was paying attention. He wouldn't have looked out of place in a gang.

Chapter 17

"Well, gentlemen," said Boyko on his return, "I hope that was helpful. Now I've arranged for Staff Sergeant Harry Cameron to talk to you. He's an expert in Chinese organized crime. Been working gangs for thirty years—spent time in Toronto and then came back to Vancouver. Oh, here he is now."

A lanky man with salt-and-pepper hair pulled into a slick ponytail and light eyes that changed colour depending on what he wore walked into the room. He was in a black t-shirt and jeans, and his eyes were stone grey as he stared around the room. Perhaps that piercing look was what had earned him the nickname "Hawk." He took a few extra seconds staring at Davis, and the two men silently compared scars. The jagged line running down the left side of Cameron's face looked deeper and was longer than the mark above Davis's right eye. Davis thought it was probably the remnant of an undercover assignment gone wrong. He smiled to himself, maybe their paths had crossed.

Boyko made quick introductions, then excused himself. Cameron slouched into the nearest chair, put one foot up on the crossbar beneath the table and leaned back. Davis wouldn't have been surprised if the guy pulled a cigarette from behind his ear and lit up right there in the conference room. Cameron may have been thinking along the same lines. He ran his tongue over his teeth for a moment, then took a foil pack of gum from his jeans pocket, popped out two pieces and shoved both in his mouth at once. Davis was pretty sure it was Nicorette.

Cameron chewed for a few moments, then shoved the wad to the side of his mouth like it was tobacco and said, "Boyko's told me a bit about what you're dealing with. He wants me to fill you in on the Chinese problem."

Lossan raised an eyebrow, which seemed to make Cameron smile. The staff sergeant leaned forward. "Fact is, the triads are the most significant criminal threat facing our country. And if you don't believe me, ask our counterparts in the US. They see them as a bigger threat than the Mexican drug cartels, the mafia or any European mobs."

Lossan nodded. "We were just down in Juarez looking into a Mexican cartel that's gone to ground. Trying to figure out how they link with these triads."

Cameron scratched his scruffy cheek. "Boyko mentioned a dead banker. Sounds like he was in deep and"—he gestured one finger across his throat—"they dealt with him."

Bolton shifted in his chair. "His name was Bob Stuart. He was a good mate. We reckon the cartel pressured him to launder for them."

Cameron looked at the well-dressed, clean-cut man in front of him. Probably a banker too. "Sorry. But they must have had something on him."

Lossan nodded. "Unfortunately, Mr. Stuart had gambling debts."

"Yep," Cameron said loudly. "That's one way they do it. And they're experts at exploiting the holes in our border. The Big Circle Boys have money laundering and casino infiltration down to a fine art."

Bolton looked up from his legal pad. "Sorry, the who?"

"Big Circle Boys. They're a triad based out of Hong Kong and Macau, and now they've imported their underground banking system here."

Lossan leaned forward. "From what we're hearing, they launder drug money, then reinvest in things like real estate and make even more money."

"That's right," Cameron said. "And to make things worse, just as we started targeting Asian organized crime groups, the federal government reduced regulatory controls at our ports." He shook his head and huffed. "Government funding cuts. You know the story."

There was a moment of head nodding around the room. Cameron got up to grab a coffee from the sideboard, seemed to think better of it, and sat back down empty-handed. "So now, organized crime groups pretty much run our ports. They bring in drugs, stolen cars... We're dealing with cargo theft and human trafficking. And all that has gotten worse in the last decade because security's a joke. And everybody knows it."

Lossan looked uncomfortable. Davis, however, was starting to think Cameron might be useful. He seemed to know exactly what was going on and didn't mind saying it out loud.

"What makes it even harder," Cameron continued, "is some of those gang members are now Canadian residents. That means it's easier for them to operate inside our borders. There's over a thousand Big Circle Boys operating in Canada, and we figure at least twenty per cent are Canadian citizens."

Lossan's brow was still wrinkled. "We have made some progress at the borders—"

Cameron cracked a grin. "An RCMP lifer. I like that. And I respect your indignation. But the fact is, the Canadian border service is useless. The Boys use their fake IDs and documents and waltz right in." He put his hands up before Lossan could interrupt. "Sure, sure, there was a recent Canadian sting, and we arrested thirty of them, including two gang bosses. So I guess that's progress."

Lossan looked a little relieved. Davis couldn't help smiling at him. In his books, the criminals would always be one step ahead. And the good guys would always be chasing them with fewer resources.

"To compound things, the Canadian refugee policy has been a problem for years," Cameron continued. "Anyone entering our country who claims to be a refugee gets a hearing, even if they have no documentation. This opened the door for the Big Circle Boys to expand their human smuggling. They traffic women from Asia and run sex rings in the US. We've saved lots of trafficked women and kids as young as seven."

Bolton looked a little pale. He hated the world his kids were growing up in. Vancouver was changing and not for the better. He doubted it would ever go back to the way it was when he first arrived in Canada. He wondered if this was why he'd agreed to continue to work on this case despite the risks. It might not be much, but perhaps his small bit would make a difference in someone's life.

"One guy claimed he was a refugee, but the bastard owned three homes in Vancouver and, get this, a luxury car dealership. He was into illegal gambling, heroin, smuggling, credit card fraud, even weapons trafficking. Immigration held him for months, but there wasn't sufficient evidence to deport him."

Lossan had pursed his lips. This was just the kind of thing that maddened him. Cameron looked directly at him.

"Don't worry. We got the bastard. We raided his home and found passports, weapons and a nice store of raw heroin." He smiled at Lossan. "We Mounties always get our man."

Lossan wasn't sure if he was teasing him. But he had to respect Cameron. The man knew his stuff. And got things done.

Cameron stood up and walked past the coffee counter again. This time he leaned over the garbage can and spit his wad of gum into it. He wiped his mouth with a napkin before saying, "Trouble is, the gang's business model keeps changing, but the flow of cash and contraband is the same."

Bolton shook his head. Cameron turned to him. "It's hard to believe isn't it. These guys have found ways to launder everywhere. They buy restaurants for cash with drug money. And we've seen them go between restaurants, casinos and underground betting houses at all hours of the day and the night. Always carrying suitcases."

"But the casinos seem to play a special role," Bolton said.

Cameron nodded. Maybe this guy was more than just a pretty face in a fancy suit. "That's right. Drug traffickers like to conduct money exchanges in casinos. If we ever stop them, they simply use the casino as an excuse for all the money they're carrying."

Chapter 18

Cameron gave up his battle and poured himself a coffee. It was two in the afternoon, and he knew he'd be up half the night. But what the hell.

Bolton set his pen down. "I just can't figure how Bob got mixed up with the Sinaloa cartel in the first place."

Cameron grunted. "I can't say I've come across any of your Mexican friends. I've got my hands full with the Chinese gangs. They've taken over the Downtown Eastside. Heroin shipments have gone crazy in the past decade. Addicts love China white. It's pure and much cheaper than the Mexican brown. Overdoses are out of control. An ER doc told me once that HIV infections have tripled in the past few years."

Cameron set his empty mug on the table and looked around at them all. "I just need everyone to understand what I'm talking about. When you have masses of people living in makeshift tents, everything they own in a shopping cart, hustlers and traders haggling over stolen goods—there's not much to look forward to. Addicts shoot up and alcoholics drink hand sanitizer."

He grimaced. "Most people don't get it. Not even cops. Unless you've worked down there."

"Sounds like a war out there," Bolton said.

Cameron nodded. "The paramedics who work in the area actually get war-zone training."

Davis had been away from the city for a long time. Sure there were drugs back in his day but nothing like this. It seemed that there was no law and order anymore, more like gang warfare. He liked to think there used to be some sort of code of conduct among the gangs, but he knew he was kidding himself. But this, well it was on another level altogether. He remembered telling his old boss that he needed to change, start using professionals to help manage the money and invest. But even he had to admit he never saw something like this coming.

Cameron shook his head. "You know there's just six blocks separating Vancouver's luxury condo towers from the Downtown Eastside."

Lossan cleared his throat. "I haven't worked the Eastside, but I've heard the horror stories. Sex workers disappearing. Addicts everywhere—on the streets, in alleys, in the parks. Hustlers exchanging cash for drugs in broad daylight."

"The place robs people of their humanity," Cameron said. "And not just the junkies, it's even the cops."

Lossan stood up abruptly and walked to the sideboard. He took a pastry from the plate and took his time turning to the room. All eyes were on him. Davis almost felt sorry for him. He looked a little lost. After decades in the service, he was still as idealistic as ever. But some of his cheerful demeanour was gone. The big officer sighed and took a bite of his pastry.

"I'm not saying the cops are dirty," Cameron clarified. "I mean they've seen too much. These cops watch people slowly die and there's nothing they can do. They know where the drugs are coming from, but they can't plug all the holes. It would drive anyone crazy."

Lossan had seen the blankness in his friends' eyes when they talked about working the Eastside. It became too hard to care about everyone they saw. They had to get their jobs done.

Cameron shifted in his seat. "I may not know a lot about the Mexican connection, but one of my best cops does. A guy named Charlie Patel," Cameron continued. "He's a sucker for sad cases, and even he's desensitized to the brutality." He shrugged. "You gotta be a wolf to catch a wolf."

Davis almost nodded. This cop knew what he was about. Davis could respect that.

"The supply of drugs is bottomless," Cameron continued. "You could put a dealer in jail and ten street kids would be waiting to fill his spot." Cameron glared around the room like he was challenging someone to argue with him. "It used to be Hells Angels dominating the marijuana market. But new gangs have moved in. And Patel says the cartels like working with the Circle Boys because those guys blend in better than the Angels or the Sicilians. A 270-pound guy wearing a skull patch on his leather jacket, well he tends to stand out. But a 150-pound guy who looks like an accountant and drives his kids to piano lessons, no one notices him."

"Maybe we could meet with this Patel," Lossan said. "Get a bit more firsthand info."

Cameron nodded. "I think I can arrange that." He stood up and stretched. "There's another thing you should know … they threaten judges, lawyers, even cops. Anyone can be eliminated by paying a gunman fifty thousand. Which is pocket change to these gangs. They fly someone in from Hong Kong, hand him a gun in a Richmond parking lot, and he's on a flight back to China before we can zip up the body bag."

A gloom seemed to settle over them. The unspoken thought being, *How do we stop these guys?* Bolton looked up and watched Lossan finishing his third donut. He wondered how his friend could eat anything. The conversation was making him feel sick. Lossan licked his fingers and finished his coffee. He set his mug down in the silence. The guy was always so gung-ho, but even he looked despondent.

Chapter 19

Superintendent Boyko looked around the room and wondered if this group would be up to taking on what he thought of as "the casino problem." His eyes stayed on Davis for a long time. He wasn't sure exactly what the ex-gangster could offer. When Davis caught him staring, Boyko cleared his throat and shifted his gaze to the door where an RCMP officer was lingering. He gave a little wave, and Boyko motioned for him to come in.

"Staff Sergeant Tom Haddock ran the force's human resource unit, handling informants, police agents and witnesses. He also ran an anti-money laundering unit task force team—that is, until his card was marked." Davis expected Boyko to elaborate on the last comment, so did Lossan and Bolton by their reaction.

Haddock walked over to greet them, and Lossan noticed the man had a slight limp. When they shook hands, Lossan towered over the man but was surprised by his strong grip. The guy couldn't have been much over five foot nine but was well built and obviously lifted weights. He reminded Davis of a large bulldog.

Boyko poured himself a coffee and took a donut as everyone settled around the table. "Tom, let's cut to the chase. Your guys spent time working the casinos. What can you tell us?"

Haddock looked around at everyone as if sizing them up. "It's a complete shitshow," he said finally.

Davis smiled. He liked this guy's style.

"Outside of federal prison, Vancouver's casinos have the highest concentration of gangsters in the province," Haddock continued. "But we've never had a plan to target organized crime in the casinos."

Davis and Lossan looked over at Boyko, who looked grim. It was as if he didn't want reminding.

Haddock leaned forward. "The simple truth is, our mandate was to go after the illegal casinos," he said. "The government didn't want us inside *their* casinos. The few times I tried investigating inside one, I got push-back. Long story short, the message was to stay out. You can just imagine how popular I became when I said things had to change."

Davis was a step ahead. Haddock had pissed off the wrong people. He was eager to hear about the guy's network of informants and spies. Bolton was furiously making notes.

Haddock picked up on Davis's reaction.

"Anyway, where was I? Oh yeah. One of my sources tell me plenty of well-connected Vancouver lawyers are getting rich advising the cartels on how to set up offshore companies. These lawyers piss me off to no end. I never felt bad about placing a bug in a posh leather chair in a fancy restaurant just across from the courthouse."

Davis smiled to himself. He liked Haddock. The guy would've done well in a gang. He wasn't afraid to bend the rules or piss people off.

"My network is a United Nations of Vancouver crime," Haddock continued. "You'd be amazed how many of these guys share information. Most of the time everyone is happy. That is, until someone rips off someone else's supply. Then there's shootings and the media are all over it."

He was enjoying telling his story. Was it because he hadn't been listened to in the past? It reminded Davis of Waddington.

Bolton was starting to enjoy himself too. He was getting an education on street crime. He'd often wondered if he'd made a mistake in his career choice. It wasn't that he didn't like what he did, it was just that he sometimes thought about what it would be like to be in the thick of things. Years ago he'd applied to join the Met Police in London. He'd been turned down. The cop that interviewed him could tell he was a bit of a high flyer and wouldn't have the patience to knuckle down and do real police work. The painstaking mind-destroying beat work that was necessary to be successful. And Bolton knew he didn't have the stomach for it either.

Haddock stretched his right leg and grimaced.

"The leg still bothering you?" Boyko asked.

Haddock shrugged. "Ten years now."

"Tom took a bullet on a drug bust gone bad," Boyko told them.

"It's worse since I been stuck at a desk," Haddock muttered.

Lossan raised an eyebrow. "At a desk? Aren't you—"

Haddock gave him a sardonic smile. "Out there? Nah. They pulled me two years ago. I think I pissed off a few too many people." He pushed himself out of his chair and walked to the side table. The group waited as he picked up a mug, poured himself a coffee and took his time surveying the donuts. Finally he took one and settled back into his seat.

"There's an unwritten rule in the casinos," he said between bites of donut. "It's called the 'no-hassle policy.' Chinese VIP baccarat players aren't required to go through the metal detectors, even though most of them are armed. The casinos are smart enough to ignore their bodyguards too. Management tells the staff that the VIPs and their entourage have been vetted. That they're all decent people."

"I take it that's not the case," Lossan said.

Haddock nodded. "These guys fly under the radar. One VIP that regularly came up on my screen was Hong Kong royalty. We know he has connections with the triads, but we can't touch him."

Bolton stopped writing and tilted his head. He looked like he wanted to ask something but wasn't quite sure how to phrase it.

Davis leaned back in his chair and placed a foot up on the crossbar. It was the same old thing, from what he could tell. Grease a few palms, you can get away with anything.

"And those are the legal casinos. Imagine how hard it is to track down and raid the illegal ones." Haddock glared at them.

Boyko cleared his throat. "Give us a bit of a rundown on those illegal places, Tom."

"Underground casinos are everywhere—all over Burnaby and East Vancouver, most run by the Big Circle Boys, Hells Angels or the mob."

Bolton was shocked. He lived in North Burnaby. This was way too close to home.

"That doesn't make them easy to find ... but once in a while we catch a break," Haddock said. "A few months back we raided a South Granville mansion and found an illegal casino and eight Malaysian women working as prostitutes. One was selling her body to pay off gambling debts. We connected the casino to a human trafficking and sex ring in Asia. Our report on the loan sharking rings and money laundering should have made a request for increased resources to go after gangs a slam dunk." He looked around at them. "But it didn't."

Bolton shook his head as Haddock continued. "That's quite an exclusive neighbourhood. Just up the street from two posh private schools."

Davis was trying to figure out who was controlling things. Was it the police or the politicians? It gave him a few ideas. He was about to ask a question when Haddock started talking again.

"We're seeing more violence every day. Even in the suburbs and other places you wouldn't expect to see it. A lot of it comes from loan sharks. These guys aren't messing around when they want their money. We've found macheted bodies dumped on wasteland. And they don't just target adults. One guy owed three hundred grand. When he couldn't pay, they grabbed his kids. Luckily a neighbour saw the kids being forced into the trunk of an SUV and called the police."

Haddock looked sickened as he told them, as though he blamed himself for what was happening. He leaned toward the table. "We had a casino employee abducted outside his home, thrown into a car with a hood over his face. He was pistol whipped, stabbed and dumped."

Bolton was holding his breath. If he'd ever thought he shouldn't get involved and help the police, all his doubts evaporated. This was his town, his life and his family.

Haddock nodded at him, like he could read his mind. "Makes you want to do something, doesn't it." He sounded wistful. "I used to feel that way..." Haddock stretched his sore leg again. "I was pretty idealistic back then." He was quiet for a moment, staring at some unknown past they couldn't see.

The guy had trodden on a few toes and pissed off too many people. And it sounded like it cost him a lot. Bolton figured he'd have probably done the same thing.

Davis leaned back in his chair. The bulldog had been sidelined. Ran into a wall of politicians. He'd probably been told to back off, but the guy couldn't do that. In his experience that usually didn't end well.

"You're still making a difference, Tom," Boyko said.

Haddock shrugged. He didn't look convinced. "Anyway, the boss here keeps me busy." He looked over at Boyko. "And I know where all the bodies are buried." He looked away again.

Haunted, Bolton thought.

Haddock let out an audible breath, then stood up and grabbed his coat from the back of his chair.

Davis was disappointed with the way things had turned out for Haddock, but he knew he'd be a great resource. He noticed a glint in Haddock's eye as he shook hands, as if he was saying, *I'll see you again.* Bolton's face was still red with rage as he said goodbye, and Lossan looked as if the job he'd taken on might be too much for him.

After he had left, Boyko looked at them. "Tom's one of the good guys. Unfortunately, he's a political casualty. Part of our job is dealing with the politicians. Sometimes we must … kiss ass. That's not everyone's cup of tea, mine included."

...

That evening at home Bolton discussed his day with his wife. There were no secrets between them, and he wanted to make sure she was comfortable with his decision to assist the police in the investigation. He told her what he'd heard that day about how gang crime, drugs and money laundering had changed the city and what the cops had to deal with every day. He told her he was going to visit the Downtown Eastside to get a firsthand look at the drug problem and that it might bring them closer to finding out what happened to Bob Stuart.

Later, as he got into bed, Bolton realized that he hadn't been exactly honest about why he wanted to be involved with the investigation. He was bored with his job. He hadn't been involved in a criminal case in years. And it wasn't just the routine work.

He didn't feel like he was affecting anyone's life in any important way. None of it really mattered. So maybe the was his chance to make a real difference.

Chapter 20

The following day, Lossan, Bolton and Davis met Charlie Patel, the cop Cameron had told them about. All of them were seated in a small coffee shop just off East Hastings Street in Vancouver's Downtown Eastside. When Lossan introduced Davis and Bolton, he could tell Patel was a little surprised at a forensic accountant being part of the team. When he told him one of the angles they were following up was money laundering, he understood.

As they were drinking their coffees, Patel nodded and looked out the window toward a rundown motel across the street. Near the front door, five or six guys were hanging around. Another stumbled into the alley next to it and was gone from sight. Lossan stared hard into the narrow dim alley, but the man didn't re-emerge.

"Homelessness is rampant around here—a lot of that started when funding was cut for low-income housing," Patel said. "Mix in the drugs and mental health problems, and you have a recipe for disaster. That's what's happened here. The gangs have simply taken advantage of the opportunity."

"There's just so many…" Bolton hadn't touched his coffee. He couldn't stop staring at the misery on the other side of the glass.

"They can rent a small room," Patel said. "They share a kitchen, toilet and bathroom. The units are tiny, maybe sixty square feet. But it's better than the street."

"I haven't been down here in a while," Lossan admitted. "It seems ... a lot worse. I don't remember so many people just ... lying on the corners. They all look strung out."

Patel nodded. "They *are* strung out. If you haven't been here for a while, what you've missed is a neighbourhood sliding into a dark crack in the earth. Most of the legitimate businesses are long gone. This is what the drug trade has done to our city."

Davis sipped his coffee. Nothing had prepared him for the changes in the city since he'd left. No one could explain the kind of tragedy he saw on Main Street and along Hastings. There were people everywhere, staggering, scratching, shouting at no one. Skinny women in filthy clothing standing on corners, waiting for their next john, just enough to pay for their next hit. People sleeping with their legs in the road, their faces against the concrete.

Bolton made a mental note to bring his kids down here one morning, preferably in the company of Patel. It would be an eye opener and make them appreciate how bad some people had things and what a privileged life they had. One day they'd remember the visit, and hopefully the lesson would last them a lifetime and help them make the right choices.

Patel looked at each of them. "It's a lot to take in. But ... look there." He pointed down the street where a bright mural enhanced the side of a building. "See her?" He nodded toward a woman in jeans, a hoodie and clean sneakers. She was carrying a basket, stopping occasionally to talk to one of the men and hand out sandwiches. "People here haven't given up," Patel said. "That's why I stay, why I'm here every day, doing what I do. If they won't give up on their home, how can we?"

Bolton shifted in his seat so he could see farther down the street. Patel was right. There were people sharing a joke, a man walking a dog. The sides of buildings were covered in artwork, some of it quite beautiful. But in the next five minutes, as they sat and drank their coffee, they also witnessed two men screaming and shoving each other. One pulled a knife and the other took off into an alley. The knife wielder followed.

Lossan stood up as if to lend assistance, but Patel touched his arm.

"This happens all the time. One of our guys will be here shortly. I'm more interested in that dealer on the corner." Patel nodded toward a skinny man in a faded plaid shirt, torn jeans and runners. "He might have some answers for you. Wait here." Patel slid out of the booth and left the coffee shop, crossed the road and headed over to the dealer.

The pair of them nodded to each other, then Patel followed the dealer around the corner and into an alley. Lossan glanced at Davis and Bolton, but they stayed where they were. They didn't want to spook the guy. Ten minutes later, Patel rejoined them in the coffee shop.

"So?" Lossan asked before Patel had taken his seat again.

"The guy was twitchier than usual," Patel told them as he slid into the booth. "He kept looking over his shoulder."

"But did he have anything?" Lossan asked.

"Says they had to waste a guy. Some banker. Sounds like it was your man, Stuart. Seems he was going to talk."

Bolton clenched his jaw. He wasn't looking forward to what he might have to tell Jani.

"And you were right. He says the Mexicans are worried. The banker's death blew a big hole in their network," Patel continued. "With the bank investigating, the cartel is shifting their operation, at least until things die down."

Davis wondered how good the informant's information really was. In his experience you never relied on just one source. You always checked it out. Who was the dealer and who was paying him? It was one thing for the cop to have good sources. But dealers came and went and rarely could they be relied on to give the straight goods. And the wrong intelligence wasted time chasing down blind alleys.

Suddenly there was a commotion outside the window. A cop car rolled to a stop a few metres from the alley where the two men had earlier been fighting. An ambulance was parked across the street. The EMS guys were on the sidewalk tending to a man who was lying on the ground. Several other men were milling around watching, but when they saw the cops, they turned and headed the other way.

"Come on. Let's go for a walk," Patel said, throwing a twenty on the table.

They left the coffee shop, passed the cop car and crossed Cordova, then turned right on Powell. Davis remembered the area well. Although he couldn't remember spending much time on foot. The farther east they walked, the more depressing it became. Addicts stumbling across streets, oblivious to traffic. Hookers looked half starved, and young kids—boys and girls who couldn't have been more than eleven or twelve—lingered on corners and in doorways. They walked past a soup kitchen line-up where most of the men looked to be in their fifties and sixties.

Patel noticed Bolton staring. "Those guys in the line-up? Some of them aren't even thirty. Most won't make it to forty. Once you end up on the street, the odds of getting out aren't good. Life expectancy around here is less than ten years." Patel nodded toward a kid squatting in a doorway. "Twelve years old and dealing. Most are working for the Angels. All of them on drugs."

They crossed the street and headed back. They noticed more and more tents on the sidewalk. A small park was full of them. Nearby, people huddled over dirty barbecues and shopping carts.

"It's best not to stare. Not to engage," Patel told them.

Bolton turned his attention to the road ahead, but it was hard to ignore the calls of the women they passed, not to feel the jaded glares.

Suddenly Patel stopped. "I see someone. He might be able to tell us a bit more. Cross the street and keep walking. I'll meet you back here in fifteen minutes."

Patel was big, but the guy he approached was three inches taller and forty pounds heavier. Davis wondered if this was Stan, the guy Patel had told them about, who commanded eighty soldiers in a First Nations gang that enforced Eastside drug debts.

Davis wondered if his past would catch up with him as he walked the east end streets. Would someone recognize him? He was more worried about a beat cop than some gangster. Gangsters had a shorter shelf life than cops. He made a note to remind Lossan that he needed to come clean with these guys before they heard it from some cop. He didn't care if it were some two-bit gangster. He could handle that. Besides it was a long time ago, and he doubted a gangster would recognize him. A cop might be different. They tended to remember a face, especially someone with a reputation.

Twenty minutes later, Patel showed up at their rendezvous point. "I've got some news. But wait till we're back in the vehicle." Patel looked over his shoulder. "And maybe we split up. You know where we're parked?"

Lossan and Davis nodded. Bolton was staring at someone across the street, but when they started walking, he followed along. He hadn't walked this area in years. Sure he'd driven down Powell Street from time to time, and even then he was scared to stop. He remembered years ago, driving east on his way home to Burnaby, there were always addicts crossing the street oblivious to oncoming traffic. They'd walk straight across the road. He'd never driven more than twenty-five miles an hour and was always ready to stop.

Ten minutes later, they met up with Patel near the corner of Powell and Cordova next to the police station, where his squad car was illegally parked. As they settled into the cruiser, Patel updated them.

"That's the second guy who told me the Mexicans have moved their money out of the bank. They acted fast. And it's what you thought. They're using the Big Circle Boys."

They said goodbye to Patel and drove on in silence for a while, leaving the chaos behind. They cut across town, past open greenspaces and mansions with lush gardens and Queen Elizabeth Park, with its lovely rolling hills, beautiful gardens and wonderful lookout points of the city and the North Shore Mountains. Then along streets with low-rise apartments and a mix of gourmet coffee shops, doctor and dentist offices and a variety of boutique high-end clothing stores. *It's like another world*, Bolton thought, staring out the window at parents proudly pushing babies in buggies and kids running in a playground with swings and merry-go-rounds. And yet it was only a few miles from streets of desperation, where lives were measured in months, and people survived on drugs.

Lossan dropped Bolton off at the Heather Street parking lot and then drove Davis back to his hotel. They pulled into the Executive Inn, and Lossan stopped by the front door. "I'll call you tomorrow. Hopefully we'll get a better picture once we have a bit more info coming in from Patel's guys."

Davis took a moment before answering. "It's not gonna bring Bolton's banker friend back though, is it?"

Lossan sighed. "Bolton is hoping for some kind of justice for his friend, for his family. But that's not a priority right now." Lossan looked grim. "We're going after the Mexican cartel."

Chapter 21

The following day, Bolton and Lossan met at Heather Street. Davis was late. Or maybe he'd decided not to join them. Lossan knew Davis wasn't sure if there was any point in his being there.

Lossan glanced across the boardroom table at Bolton, who'd been staring out the window for the past ten minutes. Probably wondering how the world they'd seen yesterday could exist with the same world he and his family lived in, not so many miles away.

Lossan stood up when his boss entered the boardroom.

"So, Corporal," Holliday said, "after all this intelligence, are you any further ahead?"

"Sir, I-I might need your help convincing Davis to join us…"

"Corporal?"

Lossan blew out his breath. "He needs a bit of prodding. He doesn't see how he can help us in the investigation."

"Mr. Davis doesn't strike me as short on confidence, and I understood he was a bit of a hit with some of our people."

"You're right on both counts, sir. I think he needs someone to reinforce the message, someone with seniority."

Holliday had learned that there were always two sides to every argument, and his experience taught him that the very act of engaging and listening to parties that often felt they'd been ignored made a difference. He'd spent years studying criminal behaviour. Placing himself inside the mind of the criminal nearly always helped provide answers. Davis was the next best thing.

Almost on cue there was a knock on the door and Davis walked in. He claimed he'd overslept, and the grey stubbled chin and creases on his face suggested it may have been true.

"So, Mr. Davis, Lossan here tells me you're not sure how you're going to fit in with our little group," said Holliday.

Davis glanced at Lossan before answering. "I'm not much use. I think you have all the resources you need."

"Well, one can never have enough resources," Holliday said. "Always plan for the unexpected, I say." Holliday looked from Davis to Lossan. "Why don't you both bring me up to speed."

Lossan sighed. "Patel has a lot of connections, but we haven't learned anything new. They're hearing the same chatter. Stuart was likely killed because he was involved in money laundering—"

"But the drugs are still coming in."

Davis rolled his eyes. "These guys are making way too much money to stop their operation because one bank is compromised."

Lossan cleared his throat. "Yes, sir. And we know the cartel's connection, this guy Alarez, is still around. Since the cartel have abandoned EFT Bank, Patel thinks they might be using the triads to launder their drug money."

"Sounds like one big happy family," Davis said.

Bolton couldn't help sighing out loud, and everyone looked at him. "Well, I can't be the only one wondering what we're supposed to do with this never-ending problem. Their bank operation gets shut down, so they just find another way to move their drug money…"

"The snake that keeps growing new heads?" Davis said. "Yeah. It's not gonna be easy. But if it was me, I'd go straight at this thing. I'd hit them where the money is."

"Are you suggesting we go after the triad, the Big…" Bolton looked down at his notes. "Big Circle Boys?"

"Eventually," said Davis. "But hitting the cartel's supply chain would be my first move. No drugs, no cash."

"So that's what a gangster would do, eh, Mr. Davis," Holliday said.

The two men started at each other for a moment. Then Davis turned to Lossan. "Your DEA friend, maybe he can be of some use. We get the Americans involved, and they'll take notice."

Holliday looked mildly offended that his own outfit wasn't enough to scare the cartel into changing plans.

Davis broke the silence. "You people need to start thinking outside the box," he said, shaking his head. "You're getting squat done sitting around, having all these meetings. You need to get dirty."

Holliday wasn't sure what to make of Davis. Clearly he had no respect for the law or the fact that police actions could be investigated and evidence thrown if it was illegally obtained. Not to mention the repercussions that would come his way once the thing fell apart. But he was intrigued.

Davis carried on. "Or maybe the answer's right in front of us…"

"What do you mean?" Lossan asked.

Davis shrugged. "Waddington knows a lot more. He doesn't just have a hunch. He's got hard evidence from the lottery corporation. People on the take—no one is doing this for free."

"How did he get the information?"

"Who cares."

"That may be illegal, Mr. Davis," Holliday said sharply. "Mr. Waddington cannot *steal* information for us."

Davis sat back. "You asked me what I'd do. I'm telling you. I don't care how he got the information."

Holliday pursed his lips. "The information must be obtained legally. Otherwise, there's no point."

"Or maybe there is," Davis argued, leaning forward. "Even just the rumour of what's going on would make a difference. You get the word out there that government officials are on the take, that Mexican drugs are taking over the city, that Chinese gangs are using Vancouver casinos like a bank—people will take notice."

Lossan looked between the two men. Nobody seemed to know what to say.

Finally, Holliday sighed. "You're not wrong. People should know what's going on. And they will. But we do this wrong, we'll spook them. They'll change tack again. Go underground. We need to keep this quiet until we have definitive proof."

Davis leaned back, shaking his head. This pen pusher was pissing him off. Unlike his undercover operation in Montreal, where the two cops running the operation had a vested interest in the outcome, all he had was a fraud cop who'd stumbled upon something too big to handle. Even the guys who worked for Boyko weren't committed to the project. And they didn't even know his background. Once that happened, Lossan would be on his own.

Davis hadn't given up completely but knew that soon he'd be headed back east. "What you need is firepower. Take the war to them. But that's just not Canada's way and you know it. The Americans must think we're a bunch of pussies, letting the triads take over our country."

Holliday frowned. Davis was a handful. He looked over at Lossan, who was smiling. "You find this funny, Corporal?"

"Sorry, sir. I was just thinking back to a conversation with a couple of RCMP officers in Montreal years ago. They planned to have Mr. Davis infiltrate a Montreal gang. But some of the things he wanted the force to do ... well, let's just say they were extreme."

"Yes, I had a conversation with an Inspector Vincent in Montreal." Holliday turned to Davis. "Didn't you propose they firebomb the gang's nightclubs and their clubhouse?"

Davis laughed. "That's the difference between you and them. I don't think the Big Circle Boys or the cartel have a code of conduct. Those guys would murder their own brother if necessary."

Holliday rubbed a finger under his chin. "I suppose if we can definitively link the cartel to the triads, then getting the US involved could work..."

"Waddington can make that connection," Davis insisted. "If he names names, well Lossan here can do some digging, get the evidence you need."

Chapter 22

Davis was standing outside, trying to shelter from the rain, when Lossan pulled into the driveway of the Executive Inn a few days later. The big corporal was all smiles. Haddock, Cameron and Patel had agreed to meet them again. Though at Davis's insistence, Waddington had not been invited. They were headed downtown to meet Bolton before their meeting out in Langley with Boyko and his team.

As they reached the freeway, they passed the Grand Villa. In a previous life, Davis had stayed there a few nights. The mattresses hadn't been replaced in years, and most of the food reminded him of reheated Chinese takeout. He knew the owners didn't care. Since they'd put in the casino, that's all that mattered. Back then, he'd spent half an hour one evening walking through the casino. He was amazed at how busy the place was. And the smell. Everyone smoked. Everywhere, people were chattering, laughing and gambling. Most of the slot machines were used. The private baccarat rooms were full. He watched a few of them gamble. At first, he had trouble figuring out what was going on. A guy would gamble for ten minutes, order a drink, pass a few turns— and then suddenly he'd gather his chips, stand up and leave the room, presumably to the cage to exchange his chips for cash.

Looking back on it, it now made sense. He also remembered the feeling of being watched. He couldn't pin it down, but he had a sense that he was noticed. He wasn't the only one just walking around the casino.

"Listen, I think we need to tell everyone about Waddington," Lossan said, drawing Davis back to the present. He pulled his vehicle into the parking lot at the Pinnacle Hotel Harbourfront where they were meeting Bolton for breakfast.

Davis got out of the vehicle and they headed into the restaurant. Working with Lossan had its ups and downs. He was completely trustworthy, of that Davis was sure. But he also trusted anyone with a badge, and that wasn't so great.

Bolton was already seated at a table. Each of them ordered before Lossan tried again. "Davis, I mean it. We need Waddington involved if this is going to work."

Davis set his coffee down. "We're talking about a man's life."

That ominous warning fell between them, and Bolton looked up from his eggs. "They'll go after Waddington."

Davis shrugged. "Waddington knows what's going on inside casinos. If it was me … I'd deal with him. Problem solved." Davis took a sip of coffee while the other two stared at him.

Lossan cleared his throat. "Obviously Waddington's key to any casino investigation. Without him, it goes nowhere. So let's make sure nothing happens to him."

"What makes you so sure he'll agree to help?" Bolton asked.

"He's itching to change things," Lossan said. "You were there, you heard him. Besides he's a cop, isn't he?"

"Was a cop," Bolton added.

Davis smirked. "Once a cop, always a cop."

Bolton ran a hand through his blond hair. "And you reckon one of Boyko's guys might be bent and tip off the cartel to deal with Waddington?"

Davis smiled. "You're catching on."

Bolton narrowed his eyes. He didn't like the way Davis treated him as if he was still wet behind the ears. But he knew it was more for effect than anything. Davis had a way of getting under people's skin. As if he didn't care. He probably didn't care.

Bolton wondered what sort of cop Davis would have made in another world. He didn't have to think much. He'd have been the sort of cop that got fired for disobedience, witness intimidation, maybe even falsifying information. It didn't bear thinking about. "You really don't trust anyone."

"That's right," Davis said. "But you're not thinking it through. It may not even be one of Boyko's team. These guys talk to their buddies. You know, over a beer. So who knows who else is in the know. There's no control over that, no matter what anyone says. My motto is 'trust no one'."

"You must have trusted the cops in Montreal," Lossan said.

"I knew the job always came first and I knew I was expendable. Waddington's gonna figure that out for sure. He needs someone that's got his back, that's all I'm saying."

"Did the guys in Montreal have your back?"

Davis thought about it. "Probably not. I knew I was the one taking all the risks. But after a while, you're in too deep and there's no going back."

. . .

When they got to Tall Timbers, Lossan left Bolton and Davis in the boardroom and headed to the front desk. He'd been waiting to hear if any of the US police departments he'd contacted had news about Landy. He called his office, and the news wasn't what he'd hoped for. Oregon State Police had found a burnt-out camper van in a national state park near Cannon Beach. Inside the camper were the remains of one male and one female. The bodies were burnt beyond recognition, but the campsite attendant had a copy of the camper's licence plate, booking details and a driver's licence. It was Landy.

The Oregon State Police had attached a copy of Landy's driver's licence and vehicle registration, along with a photo of the burnt-out camper, and promised to send more once the coroner and fire department had filed their reports.

Lossan asked his assistant to email a copy of the report to Boyko's attention at Tall Timbers. Then he called Boyko and gave him the news. He reminded him that they were all planning on meeting with Cameron, Patel and Haddock in half an hour and he had a favour to ask.

"Let me guess, you want me to skip the meeting?"

"Your being there may make some of your men … what's the word…"

"Restrained?"

"They all have a lot of respect for you, but you being in the room may influence their decision. They need to buy into this without you pressuring them."

"Point taken, Corporal." He cleared his throat. "Is your Mr. Davis going to be a part of this team?"

"That's depends on them," Lossan admitted. He didn't tell him that Davis was already there and had the beginnings of a plan of his own. "In any case, sir, it would help if you're there to start with and then let us kick it around with your team. We can regroup at the end if that makes sense."

Lossan hung up and walked down to the boardroom. He told Bolton and Davis the news about Landy. It took Bolton time to take it all in.

"They're confident it's arson," Lossan said. "They'll confirm the remains using dental records." He sighed. "It looks like Landy was involved somehow. What we don't know is to what extent."

Bolton's mind was racing. He wasn't focused on the *why*; he was thinking about what it meant for him and his family. Had someone been watching Landy? Did they know he'd been in touch with Landy lately? Did they know about the journal and the police investigation?

Bolton sat down. "I told Landy about the journal. What if he started digging into it and that's what got him killed." He went pale. "My god. I may have gotten that man killed."

"What?" Lossan looked alarmed at the turn his friend's thoughts were taking. "No."

But Bolton was shaking his head. "Or maybe he was tangled up in something dodgy, maybe he told his contacts about the journal and maybe they decided he was a loose end—" He looked up at them. "And maybe I am too."

"We don't know that," Lossan said. "There could be any number of reasons."

Bolton put his hand on his forehead. What had he got himself into? What was he going to tell Holly? He could hear Lossan talking, trying to reassure him. But he wasn't listening. It was too late now. Whoever murdered Landy likely knew about his involvement.

"Hey, Bolton," Davis said. His deep voice broke through Bolton's stupor. Bolton looked at him. "First of all, if this Landy character got in bed with the cartel—which I think he probably did—then he knew what he was getting into. And that's on him." Davis waited for that to sink in. "But if he was innocent and just dug around too much, well, my guess is a guy like that would have been discreet. He wouldn't have gone blasting off about his source. So stop worrying, okay?"

Somehow, hearing that from Davis calmed Bolton. The ex-gangster always seemed to know what he was talking about. Bolton felt his body relax.

Lossan was relieved his friend had calmed down, but he thought there was a good chance Davis had just lied to him. In his mind, there was every reason to believe that Landy may have talked about the journal, whether he was working for the cartel or not. Of course he'd tell them about it. And if so, Bolton could be right. Maybe they were starting to clean up loose ends.

Chapter 23

Before the others arrived in the boardroom, Davis reminded Lossan that he needed to be upfront with the rest of the group about his background.

"Leave it to me," said Lossan.

When they arrived with Boyko, Lossan stood up. "Gentlemen, thanks for coming."

Lossan waited for the men to pour coffees and sit down before he continued. He opened the file in front of him. "Now before we discuss the situation, I want to update you on two things. Firstly, charred remains of a man and woman have been found in a burnt-out camper van in Oregon. We're waiting for the autopsy report to confirm identities, but the campsite records show a driver's licence and vehicle registration belonging to Ed Landy. So it looks like Landy was either part of the cartel's operations, or the cartel decided he was getting too close and eliminated him."

Davis slowly looked at Cameron, then Patel and finally Haddock. He thought he noticed a small tremor in Cameron's left eye, just above his scar. Neither Patel nor Haddock showed any reaction.

"Secondly," Lossan continued, "we've gotten word from the DEA that a gang war has broken out at the Port of Manzanillo in Mexico. It looks like a move by the Sinaloa cartel to take over the import of meth precursors from China. The port is under the control of the

Mexican military, but there are more holes in port security than you can imagine … let's just say their policing makes Vancouver look like a model of security."

Cameron leaned forward. "I don't see us ever stopping the supply of product, whether its meth or cocaine. There's a lot more money to be made, which means more money to launder. It's all about the laundering. Shutting that down or, at the very least, making it as tough as possible, that's got to be our number one priority."

Boyko put his hand on his head, as if he had a headache. "I think it's both. Stop the product coming in and stop the money laundering." His gaze settled on Davis. "It looks as if you find this amusing, Mr. Davis."

"Not really. I was just thinking of a New York mobster in the early fifties named Frank Costello. He was asked by a committee investigating illegal gambling how they could curb gambling in the US. His answer was simple. 'Burn down the stables and shoot the horses.'"

Haddock looked confused and stared at Davis, who still had a smile on his face.

"You guys never heard of Murder, Inc.?" Davis looked around the room. "Bunch of powerful mobsters, like Lucky Luciano and Bugsy Siegel. Started during prohibition. These guys controlled the casinos and paid the cops to look the other way. They ran everything in the fifties." He shrugged. "Eventually some were deported back to Italy, some died in prison and some were shot by rival gangs."

Lossan was annoyed. He'd warned Davis about hijacking the meeting. Now he was insulting the cops before Lossan even had a chance to tell them about the ex-gangster's background. Lossan stared at him, hoping to shut him down.

"If only it were that easy." Boyko pursed his lips. Davis was implying that the police were involved in money laundering inside casinos or, at least, turning a blind eye to it. That's what Waddington had said. Somehow it seemed worse coming from the ex-con.

"Christ they even had J. Edgar Hoover in their pocket," Davis continued. "Costello blackmailed him with some naughty pictures." Davis raised an eyebrow. "You know Hoover was gay."

Lossan put his hand up like a policeman at a traffic stop, but Davis ignored the warning. "Hoover would deny the existence of a nationwide organized crime syndicate. After he died, Costello testified that Hoover would get his own agents to place huge bets on races for him. Costello was pissed at the number of races that he was made to fix on Hoover's behalf."

Davis stood up and poured himself a coffee. Lossan hoped he had finished his rant. He looked over at Boyko, wondering why he wasn't reining Davis in, but Boyko was distracted by someone at the door. He apologized to the group and said he had to take an urgent call.

Davis sat down and carried on. "Well, guess what? Nothing's changed. The casino operators are still crooks and so is anyone else who allows the laundering to continue. I'm sure they've got cops in their back pocket. And the government's filling their own pockets too. They're all a bunch of snakes."

Bolton let out an audible sigh. Davis had just insulted all three cops. Was he trying to sabotage the operation before it even got started?

"The question is, what are you guys gonna do about it?" Davis demanded, looking around the room. "All this time, you've been sitting on all this information. You need to go after these guys."

Lossan was nodding, seeing an opportunity to take over the discussion and shut down Davis. "And that's what we're going to do. We're putting a joint task force together. It'll combine security service, gang units and commercial crime. The goal is to cut off the cartel's drug supply to Canada, stop the triads from laundering the cartel's drug money and uncover EFT Bank's links to the cartel here in Canada, the US and Mexico."

Davis chuckled, and everyone turned to him again. He put up his hand in an apologetic gesture.

Lossan pursed his lips. "It's a lot, I'll give you that. But we've got a lot of good information now. And with this group, I think we have a chance." He dared Davis to disagree. But Davis only leaned back placidly and motioned for Lossan to continue.

"I think each of you could play a major role in the operation." Lossan stopped and picked up a glass of water. "Now before we begin"—he glanced at Davis—"I need to tell you about Mr. Davis."

There was silence in the room. Haddock, Cameron and Patel each stared at Davis.

Lossan took a sip of water and cleared his throat. "Years ago, Mr. Davis was involved in a major undercover operation back in Montreal. He penetrated a drug trafficking gang that controlled the port. The successful operation took over eighteen months." Lossan had decided to start with something positive. The men looked mildly impressed. So a good start.

Lossan took a little breath and blew out the next bit of information in one quick stream. "Prior to that he was in witness protection. He used to be a senior member of a Vancouver gang, run by a guy named McVittie. The gang controlled the port and most of the drugs that arrived in the city."

Lossan saw the looks on their faces and knew he'd lost them. "Mr. Davis was persuaded to assist us in shutting down a major drug operation at Vancouver's port. Most of the gang members are dead or serving time in federal penitentiaries back east."

Davis felt the gaze of each of three cops. They were looking at him differently. He wasn't one of them.

"I believe he can play a role in this operation," Lossan said. "But only if you're all onside."

Davis was amused. The cops didn't know what to say. Sure, he'd helped them put away a lot of bad guys. But most cops never saw past the tattoos and scars. Once a gang member, always a gang member.

Haddock was the first to speak. "What's his role?"

Davis grit his teeth. They were already doing it. Talking like he wasn't there. He was just an asset to be used in their investigation. He leaned back in his chair. He was beginning to regret coming back to Vancouver. He should have listened to his gut.

"Davis is a good sounding board." Lossan kept his eyes on Haddock. He could only imagine how annoyed Davis looked. "He's good at kicking holes in things, telling us what will work and what won't. He offers a gangster's perspective. Or should I say a former gangster." There he'd said it. He hadn't meant to, but Davis hadn't stayed on script, baiting the cops. Like it was his plan all along. He wondered if it sounded better coming from him rather than Davis.

"One idea is for him to be part of the lottery corporation's anti-money laundering staff. Be our eyes on the triads inside the casinos."

"You could always use an undercover cop," said Haddock. He turned to Davis. "Instead of an ex-con."

Patel nodded. "That'd be my call."

"Cameron? What do you think?" asked Lossan.

Cameron stretched out his legs and reached into his jeans pocket for his pack of Nicorette. He popped two into his mouth and chewed on them for a moment, making direct eye contact with Davis. "Well," he said finally, "I like to think we aren't stupid enough to not use someone who could be of value."

Lossan nodded. "That's my view of it as well."

Bolton cleared his throat, and they all looked at him. All they really knew about him was that he was a forensic accountant hired by the RCMP Commercial Crime group. Up until that point, no one had paid much attention to him. They were busy wrestling with the idea of including an ex-gangster. "Well, I agree," he said, mostly so they'd stop staring at him. "I've worked with Davis before. And, well, everything turned out all right in the end."

Lossan gave him an encouraging smile, then turned back to the others. "One more thing. We know the cartel has been using a guy named Alarez as their point man. I think we bring him in. From what we know, he's been operating here on behalf of the cartel for some time."

"What makes you think he's gonna tell us anything?" Haddock said.

Davis was annoyed that Lossan had mentioned Alarez in front of the whole group. The more people who knew about that, the more chance Alarez could get warned. Was he going to tell them about Waddington too? Before Lossan could answer, Davis stood up.

"That's not really the point, is it." They all watched him walk over to the side table and pour himself a coffee. "You pick him up and make sure they know about it down in Juarez, that he's squealing about the dealer network. Then you get his wife in Sinaloa arrested and sent to El Paso. Make sure everyone knows she's been picked up by the DEA."

Bolton was shocked. That meant putting Alarez's whole family in danger. He'd missed that when they'd been discussing the plan at breakfast. Judging by Lossan's reaction, he'd missed it too. Davis looked angry. Was he was making this up on the fly?

"He'll either squeal and want protection or say nothing," Davis said. "It doesn't really matter, if the cartel thinks he's talking. My guess is he'll be worried about his wife and kids." Lossan looked at the three cops, trying to read their reaction.

Haddock looked over at Davis. "You're just stirring up as much shit as you can to see what happens."

Davis shrugged. "Make them paranoid. Let them think you know more than you do."

Cameron looked like he'd gained a new respect for Davis. "The cartel may try to take out Alarez," he said between chews on his gum. "They'll figure he's given up some names."

"And he might tell us their drug routes," said Bolton. "We can begin clearing this stuff off the streets."

Cameron shook his head. "Maybe. But more likely, a guy like Alarez has lower-level info. He won't know the major players, the big fish you need to put a real dent in this thing. You can squeeze him a bit. But he's more useful to just disrupt things."

"The point is, everyone will be scrambling," Davis added. "That's when people make mistakes. Move money too quick and things get sloppy." *None of this is going to work*, he thought. *But at least they'll be distracted. They won't be thinking about Waddington.*

Haddock looked at Lossan and then Davis. "Your plan is crazy. All you're doing is creating chaos."

Charlie Patel was looking back and forth between Davis and Lossan as though watching a dress rehearsal of a poorly written play that was likely to close on opening night. And he and the other cops were being asked to sign up and be part of the disaster. Then there was the fact that one of the players was an ex-gangster they didn't know from a hole in the ground. They'd be a laughingstock inside the force. This kind of operation required careful planning, not some bullshit made up in the moment by a guy who clearly didn't care if any of them got hurt. And where was the boss? Had he signed off on this?

Patel looked at Lossan. "So what's our role in all this?"

"We need eyes on Alarez for starters," Lossan said. "You're all well connected on the street. The most important thing is going to be surveillance. Keeping your ears open. The goal here is to collect evidence. To do that, we need to know exactly how this operation works. If we can link the cartel to the triads, we can put pressure on the US to go after EFT Bank in the States. In the end, financial records are going to be how we trace the flow of money—that's how we may get these guys."

Just like Al Capone, thought Davis.

Chapter 24

Bolton had another meeting out in Surrey and told them he was going to catch a cab. Lossan was pleased. It'd give him a chance to talk to Davis on his own while they drove back into the city. He wasn't happy with the way Davis handled the meeting, but he had to tread carefully. Davis didn't seem to care what happened and wasn't afraid of upsetting anyone. He needed to try the soft approach.

"Do you really think pulling Alarez in is going to work?" Lossan asked.

Davis was staring out the window at the grey sky. "I have no idea."

"It's not a bad plan," Lossan continued, as if convincing himself. "It's a little rough around the edges, I'll give you that. But putting psychological pressure on these guys can have a real effect." He half turned toward Davis. "Who knows? Maybe a few more will come forward with information to avoid being implicated."

Davis doubted this.

"Anyway, it gives us an advantage," Lossan continued. "We're forcing them to be more cautious and less effective. It buys time so we can keep investigating." Lossan turned onto the road where Davis's hotel was. "What do you think?"

Davis shook his head. "Those guys have a problem working with me. I get that. But they're not desperate. It's not their plan—it's your plan, and that's a problem. They're just doing this because their boss asked them to."

It was still raining, and traffic was heavy. Lossan frowned. He had to admit even he wasn't sure why he was getting involved. This was more of a Security Service operation. And getting the Americans to go after the bank in the US and Mexico, well who was he kidding? It was unlikely anything would happen anytime soon with the bank. But he knew they had to try something.

Davis broke the silence. "Listen, I'm gonna stick around till the weekend, and then I'm heading back to the Maritimes." He put up a hand to stop Lossan's interruption. "Would you believe I'm going to look up my ex-wife? We have nothing in common but our daughter. After all these years, she still blames me for her going to college in New Brunswick. Well, at least Lauren moved back to BC."

Lossan didn't speak. He didn't like the idea that Davis was thinking of leaving. But it was rare that the ex-gangster spoke about anything personal.

"Her problem is she's lonely," Davis muttered.

"Your daughter?"

Davis gave him a look. "My ex. It's not my fault she's alone. She should have moved on, years ago."

When the silence stretched to a full minute, Lossan said, "Sometimes it's not that easy to move on." He glanced at Davis. "You should know that."

Davis had forgotten how much it rained in Vancouver.

"You know my daughter's talking about getting married. Wants me to come to the wedding." He turned toward Lossan with a smirk. "I wonder if she's told her future husband what I did for a living."

Lossan couldn't help smiling.

"You know what's funny," Davis continued, "the guy she's marrying is a criminal lawyer. Met him when she was doing her master's in criminology." He traced a raindrop down the window. "You never think your kids are gonna grow up. Who knows, maybe I'll be a grandfather." He sighed. "I've gotta live my own life. I'm gonna tell my ex the same thing. It's great to have kids and spend time with them, but kids grow up and move on, they start to live their own lives, raise a family—and then what do we have left?" His hand dropped into his lap. "Just memories."

"What's brought all this on?" said Lossan, squinting through the windshield.

"I've had a lot of time to think about things. I'm enjoying myself living back east. I'm even made a difference in a few lives. But…"

"Don't tell me you're lonely?" Lossan said.

Lossan waited for the answer, and after a few seconds, Davis said, "Yes, I need someone to spend time with."

Silence fell between them again. Lossan wished his wife was there. She could talk to anyone about anything. She'd know what to say. Or what not to. *Sometimes just be quiet*, she'd told him once, when he confided to her that he didn't know what to say when their teenage daughter had been upset about something at school.

"There was someone back east…"

Lossan was delighted. Being quiet worked. He'd have to tell his wife.

"But that was years ago. We lost touch."

"Why don't you look her up?"

"I brought her a lot of grief. Anyway, I'm not sure I would fit into the small town where she lives, and I know she'd never move."

"You never know." Lossan was enjoying playing matchmaker. "Maybe she's looking for someone. And maybe she's worth moving for."

Davis didn't answer.

"I mean would you rather be alone in a city or with someone in a small town?"

It was a good question, and one Davis couldn't answer in that moment.

Lossan realized now wasn't the time to take Davis to task over his attitude in the meeting. It'd probably tip him over the edge. He dropped Davis off at the Executive Inn in Burnaby.

The area had changed. Davis didn't remember all the high-rise condominium developments. And the traffic, so much traffic. He wondered about the future of Vancouver and whether he could ever move back. Or were there too many bad memories and too many ghosts?

...

When Lossan got to Heather Street, he walked straight down the hall to his boss's office. Holliday's door was open, and he tapped on it lightly.

"Come on in, Pat. I just had a call from Superintendent Boyko. It seems his guys are not too keen on Davis."

Hardly surprising, Lossan thought and then said, "Well, it wasn't a great meeting. Davis was Davis, laid it out and didn't pull any punches. He doesn't care who he pisses off. Working alongside an ex-gangster might be a challenge for those guys."

Holliday smiled and said, "I can't blame them. But good news. Boyko's persuaded them to give the boys in Montreal a call. Seems one of them is retired, but the other guy, Lacroix, is still around. I'm not sure there's much more we can do at this end. For what it's worth, and don't tell him I told you this, I think Boyko has a soft spot for Davis. He pointed out that not too many ex-cons would return to their old neighbourhood and expose themselves to God knows what sort of risks."

It was Lossan's turn to smile as he said, "Davis has that effect on people. I remember talking to the guys in Montreal a couple of years ago. One of them told me it was as if Davis was looking for something. A way to prove himself."

"A guilty conscience perhaps?" Holliday said.

Lossan shrugged. "Davis has nothing to prove. In my books, he's more than made up for his time in the gang. He could've stayed in the Maritimes, living the quiet life, but he comes all the way out here to see if he can help, and who knows … maybe he can."

Holliday was always skeptical about ex-cons turning their lives around. In his experience it rarely happened, and it wasn't through lack of trying. All too often life was stacked against them, and it took a very unusual and strong personality to turn the corner.

"You know what he's been doing back east?"

"No idea," said Holliday.

"Working at the Salvation Army. Teaching young offenders on probation how to stay out of prison."

Holliday shifted in his chair. There was always the exception.

Chapter 25

That evening Lossan took his wife out for dinner. He needed to unwind, and she'd been reminding him that the two never spent much time together. She'd put up with a lot of moves around the province when they'd been younger. Every five or six years, accepting postings up north in some small town where it got below thirty degrees and winter lasted forever. It'd been tough on the kids when they were young, especially once their friends found out that their old man was a cop. Moving back to Vancouver's North Shore had worked out. His plan was to retire when he was done his thirty years and get a job in private security. Maybe in the Alberta oil and gas industry, closer to the kids and grandchildren.

His wife was a good listener, and she never complained when he talked shop. "Sorry. It's this case. It's getting me down. It's just not going anywhere. And our guy is thinking of heading back east."

"The ex-con?"

"Yeah. He's abrasive, that's for damn sure. And, of course, the cops have trouble working with him."

"Pat, you can't solve every problem. Things don't always work out."

Lossan sighed. "Forget about my work. Tell me about our oldest. What's the problem?"

"Oh, you know Sally. Always has so much on going on. And I think she's fallen out with her boyfriend."

"Do I need to talk to her?"

"Of course you do. You know what she's like, she never talks to me. She's always been Daddy's little girl."

. . .

Lossan was late into the office the next morning. He'd just come from a meeting with Crown counsel on some commercial fraud case he'd been working on. The Crown told him there was insufficient evidence to proceed. Lossan was starting to feel like he'd been in the force too long. The job was getting tougher. The bad guys often seemed to get off on some technicality, and the courts appeared to go out of their way to suspend sentences or settle on the minimum sentence.

He needed some hobbies. He had none. He didn't exercise. Most of his friends were in the force, and whenever they met up all they did was talk shop. He needed to look to the future and find an interest. Maybe he'd touch base with some of his old Albertan buddies still in the force and find out what their plans were.

When he saw the message from Superintendent Boyko, his mood worsened. He knew it was bad news, that Haddock, Cameron and Patel had decided they didn't want to be part of an operation that involved Davis. And since it really wasn't Lossan's operation to begin with, there wasn't much he could do about it.

He walked down the hall to pour himself a coffee. He wasn't in a hurry to hear what Boyko was about to tell him. An hour later, a call from Charlie Patel turned his day around. "I've got some news about your man, Alarez," Patel said. "Word is he's been living in an apartment near the college off Oak Street. I've got a guy keeping an eye on the place. I'll call you when I hear anything more."

Lossan set the phone down and sighed. Maybe they were getting somewhere.

He went through some old paperwork, an old fraud case they'd never really done anything with. He was looking for something to take his mind off calling Boyko. Suddenly his phone rang. He didn't recognize the number, and hoping it was something new, he picked up.

"I wanted to let you know," Boyko said, "Haddock, Cameron and Patel are in." Lossan held the phone blankly. "Hello, Corporal, did you hear me?"

"Yes, sir … just surprised."

"Anyway, they called an Inspector Lacroix in Montreal. Apparently he told these guys, and I quote, 'I would trust Alan Davis before any cop I've ever worked with, and if you're too scared or too stupid to hire the guy, then maybe you should all become traffic cops.'"

Lossan grinned but stayed silent as Boyko continued. "Lacroix went on to tell them that some of Davis's ideas and methods were off the wall. But given all the circumstances, what he did in Montreal was probably the only way to go after the gang. Apparently Lacroix said he'd be willing to fly to Vancouver to explain to them why they should hire Davis." Boyko didn't sound the least bit offended. In fact, he sounded amused.

"That's great news, sir. So where do we go from here?"

"Sergeant Haddock is going call you. He's the one who convinced Patel."

"Thank you, thank you very much, sir."

Chapter 26

Davis's meeting with his ex-wife had gone better than expected. The lunch was good, and they talked mostly about Lauren, a subject that came naturally. Davis wanted to know if his ex would be comfortable with him attending the wedding. He also wanted her take on Lauren's fiancé.

Stella seemed surprised that he knew about the wedding, but then, her daughter didn't tell her everything, and clearly she was in touch with her father.

"Is this why you're back here, Alan? I mean … you're not in trouble again, are you?"

Davis waited until the waitress had cleared their plates. "No, nothing like that, but the less you know the better."

She tilted her head thoughtfully. "How come you never moved on?"

He stared at her for a moment, then glanced away. He'd always loved those hazel eyes. Lauren must have told her he was still on his own. He was surprised she'd asked. "I'm okay as I am."

Stella smiled at him. "You miss Lauren, don't you?" She was trying to make an effort, even if it was only to please her daughter.

"Of course I do." He faced her again. "There's not a day that goes by that I don't regret what happened to us. But I can't change the past."

Davis knew the only reason Stella had agreed to meet him was because their daughter had asked her to. It was time to leave. He didn't want to make it any harder for her. He signalled to the waitress and paid the bill. He was going to say, *I'll see you at the wedding*, but he knew that would only make things worse. He stood up and said goodbye.

…

When he returned to his hotel, there was a message from Lossan. Davis called him back.

"Haddock and the boys are in," Lossan said, sounding more than ever like the Lossan of years ago. Davis almost pictured him smiling. "Lacroix told them they'd be stupid not to use you."

Davis didn't say anything.

"So you'll stay, right? You'll help us out?"

Davis scratched his cheek as he thought about it. "Yeah, I'll stay."

"We need to talk to Waddington. Boyko is okay with it if Waddington agrees, but he still hasn't shared it with his guys. He isn't happy about that. Doesn't like the idea that you're suggesting they're not trustworthy."

"Too bad," Davis said flatly.

Lossan rolled his eyes. "I've arranged for Boyko's guys to meet us tomorrow afternoon at two. Bolton's coming too." Lossan sounded almost giddy. "Looks like everything's coming together," he said.

Typical Lossan. Always the optimist, way too trusting and thinking everything will be fine. Davis looked out the window. *We'll see*, he thought. He was surprised the cops had agreed to work with him. He'd been pretty set on heading back east. The sudden change in plans unnerved him. He didn't like curveballs.

Chapter 27

Since the first meeting at Tall Timbers, Boyko had been considering seeking the appointment of a special prosecutor to investigate any wrongdoings by a member of the government in connection with the casinos. Such an appointment had to be made by someone in the attorney general's office, usually the deputy. And given they might be implicating an employee who was working in the attorney general's office, he had to tread carefully.

He thought of an old friend who had acted as a special prosecutor in complicated cases in the past. Boyko decided to roll the dice. He needed some advice.

Bill Koch had a reputation for cutting though the bullshit. He'd always made it clear that while he hated crooked politicians as much as the next person, for a prosecution to stick, you needed evidence, witnesses and, most of all, luck. Koch listened to Boyko's description of the casino problem.

When the superintendent finished speaking, his friend sighed. "You don't really have much evidence, Val. You know that won't hold up in court. Or do you have anything beyond what people are saying?"

Boyko bristled a bit. "We have a man. He works at the lottery corporation. He has information on people in the corporation who know what's going on and aren't doing anything about it."

"You'll have a hard time proving that's a criminal offence. Even if you find evidence, they could claim it wasn't their problem. The RCMP should have done something."

Boyko was feeling tired. They needed to investigate to get evidence. And they needed to get evidence to investigate. "What if this guy can provide hard evidence? I mean wire transfers, account information, things that show the payoffs to lottery corporation employees."

"Legally," Koch said, "everything must be done by the book, or the court can throw it out. You of all people know the score. And, Val, you need to talk to the assistant AG. Get a sense of how cooperative they're going to be."

Boyko gritted his teeth. His old friend was right. He'd have to go into the lion's den.

When he got off the call with Koch, Boyko leaned back in his chair and stared out the window for a few minutes. He respected Davis's opinion and had kept Waddington's name out of the discussions up to now. But he'd also worked with his guys for more than ten years, and he'd always been able to count on them.

If they were going to be a team, they would have to trust one another and so would Davis.

Boyko had spent his life protecting others. He'd travelled the world, working with different security and police services, finding solutions to complicated problems involving criminal networks. He loathed dealing with politicians, but it was part of his job, and he'd often bowed to the will of the government, whether he agreed with it or not. But the city he'd worked in had gradually been taken over by sophisticated criminal networks with connections in government and the security service.

His career has cost him dearly. He was divorced, living on his own, and had little to show for his almost thirty years in the force. A two-bedroom condominium on the Fraser River in New Westminster and a pension, that was it. But the place did have a spectacular view of the river. He'd spend his spare time on the covered patio reading a book, watching the river traffic go by and researching his Ukrainian heritage.

He was comfortable on his own, having spent most of his adult life alone. He'd often been described as a workaholic. He was dedicated to his men and all of them were dedicated to him. He was fair but demanding. Often he'd listen in meetings rather than speak. But when he spoke, everyone tended to listen and not just because he was in charge.

He had few vices beyond single malt whisky. He'd risen far and fast in the force and would have gone further but for his refusal to follow political orders when he knew they were wrong. But he was looking forward to the time when he'd leave the force. He'd been approached by the private sector on a few occasions and knew that one day when the time was right, he'd make the change.

…

The next day, Charlie Patel called Lossan. "No sign of Alarez," he said. "The house is empty. My guy hasn't seen anyone in or out."

Lossan thanked him and hung up with a sigh. This was not the start he'd been hoping for. He glanced at his watch. It was almost four o'clock and he was meeting with Carlos Adriano at the airport. The DEA agent had been in Seattle for a few days on some drugs bust involving the Sinaloa cartel and flew up to Vancouver to meet Lossan for an early dinner before heading back to Texas.

An hour later, the two men sat back with glasses of red wine. Lossan told him about the Alarez development.

"We were going to ask you to pick up his family," Lossan said, "but I'm not sure there's any point if we can't find Alarez."

Adriano stroked his chin. He was wondering whether they should pick up his wife and son anyway. News of their arrest would soon get back to Alarez. That might put pressure on him to make an appearance.

Adriano had always made it clear that in order to shut down the cartel, they'd need some help from the DEA accessing intelligence from the Sinaloa cartel in Mexico. Shutting down their drug routes, eliminating their dealer network and stopping the money laundering through the casinos might not be enough. Often there were members buried deep in the organization that only the top guys in Sinaloa knew anything about. Bolton's friend Bob had probably been one of those well-guarded secrets. But were there others?

Their food arrived, and Lossan watched Adriano dig in. He looked at his own plate and wished he'd ordered something lighter.

"Someone in Sinaloa knows the Vancouver network back to front," Adriano said between bites of his wrap. "It was their brainchild. They'd have taken years setting it up. Probably lived in Vancouver for a while. Could have even been a relative of Alarez." He wiped a napkin across his lips. "It's not going to be easy to eliminate it completely."

Lossan grimaced and sipped his wine. For once, he didn't have any appetite.

Adriano took another bite and chewed for a few moments. "Have you considered, my friend, that it may not be just one triad involved in laundering for the cartel?"

Lossan nodded. "We talked about that. But figuring out how deep this goes…"

Adriano raised his eyebrows. "You didn't think this would be easy, did you?"

Lossan sighed. "Not easy, but this feels, well, almost impossible."

"Yes. Each time we have a small success and put away one bad guy, another one pops up. But this is the job, my friend."

Just like Davis said. It was a snake that kept growing new heads. This might be the job, but Lossan didn't have to like it.

Adriano placed his napkin on his empty plate and sat back. "Have you considered the timing of Alarez's disappearance?"

Lossan pursed his lips. He'd thought about this too. It couldn't be a coincidence that right before they were going to pick him up, the cartel member had gone off the grid. Davis certainly wouldn't think it was an accident. And Lossan was starting to get the feeling that he was right.

"I don't want to accuse anyone in your organization," Adriano said, "but it's not unusual for the cartel to bribe cops. I think you know this. You need to tread carefully. Trust no one."

Chapter 28

Over the next few days, Patel, Haddock and Cameron met with their contacts and watched people they suspected were involved with the cartel's operation. They didn't see one of them so much as jaywalk. Lossan was frustrated. It was as if they knew they were being watched. Even worse, Alarez was still nowhere to be found.

"He's just disappeared," Patel told them when they met on a rainy Friday afternoon at Tall Timbers. "He's definitely gone underground."

Davis grunted and drew their stares. He looked around at them all but, for once, kept quiet. He was thinking of all the people who might have known about their plan. They hadn't been careful enough. He wasn't sure if Lossan or Holliday had spoken with someone in the DEA about picking up Alarez's family. And who knows how many people in Tall Timbers had heard about what was going down. Lossan was too trusting.

"What now?" Lossan wondered. He was feeling dejected as he looked out a rain-streaked window.

The door opened, drawing their attention. Superintendent Boyko entered with Doug Waddington in tow. Lossan, who looked a little guilty, couldn't help glancing at Davis. The ex-gangster looked furious.

But Boyko wasn't about to apologize for his decision to reveal Waddington. "For those of you who don't know," he said, "this is

Doug Waddington." Waddington, who had already picked up a donut from the sideboard, smiled with his mouth full and gave a small wave with fingers that were covered in powdered sugar. He took a seat at the end of the table.

"Waddington has worked at the lottery corporation for over a year now," Boyko said. "He's seen firsthand what's going on. And he's our best source of direct evidence."

Patel stared hard at the big man, while Cameron gave him a glance then turned his attention back to Boyko.

Haddock leaned back in his chair with a steaming cup of coffee. "What sort of evidence?"

"Mr. Waddington, would you mind walking us through it?"

Waddington looked like he'd been waiting for years to tell someone about what he'd known all along. He took a moment to wipe his fingers with a paper napkin, dabbed his lips, leaving a bit of powdered sugar on one cheek, and stood up.

"Well, basically, for the past year I've been telling my bosses about the corruption in casinos. It's plain as day they're being used to launder cartel drug money. And most people know what's going on. That includes those at the top, the people walking the floors and the gamblers playing the slot machines. Anyone denying that is either lying or kidding themselves." Despite his somewhat comical appearance, Waddington's words hit home. All eyes were on him.

"But I'm ignored. My reports don't always get filed. Fact is, no one wants to lose the massive revenue coming in from these illegal operations." Waddington sat back in his chair and let that sink in for a moment.

"So," he continued, "I kept my own record. They might not file all my reports, but I still have the dirt that was in them. We can use it to go deeper, get whatever we need to make a real case against these bastards and take them all out once and for all."

The men glanced around at each other. All except Davis, who was staring at Boyko with murder in his eyes. Next to him, Lossan looked excited. Haddock was chewing on his lip. Bolton didn't know if it was from anticipation at getting closer to a win or anxiety about rooting out bad cops and politicians. People they may have worked with for years. He was also wondering what reports he was referring to.

"There's other stuff too," Waddington said. "A guy named Roberts who works in Gaming and Enforcement received two payments of a hundred grand from casinos licenced by the government. His wife was picked up in a raid of an underground casino. Turns out she owed money to loan sharks. We're talking over two hundred grand. We think Roberts was trying to find a way to pay off her debts."

Waddington shifted in his seat. "We don't know exactly what the deal was, but Roberts has been in the position to do something about money laundering for a few years and he hasn't taken any action. It's clear to me, someone bought him off."

"But you don't actually know that," Haddock stated.

Waddington shrugged. "In my view, everything's just below the surface, just waiting to be uncovered. We start digging, we're going to find a gold mine."

Bolton noticed a gleam in Lossan's eyes and it made him smile.

"And then there's my own backyard." Waddington shook his head. He went on to explain that two officers in the lottery corporation had received payments from the casino operators for "consulting services."

Haddock stared at Waddington again. "You have evidence?"

Waddington hesitated and looked at Boyko, who shuffled through some papers then handed over some documents. They included wire transfers and bank statements showing annual payments each of fifty thousand over a three-year period.

Davis's jaw tightened as he listened. Did the Crown have to disclose their information and their sources? If so, Waddington was dead. No one seemed worried about how long these things took and how exposed witnesses were until they went to court. He of all people knew that better than anyone.

Waddington was thinking along the same lines. He'd been there before, in Australia. Worried about watertight cases that had suddenly evaporated when key witnesses disappeared or refused to testify. Some had even been murdered. He was always the one promising to protect them. But he knew that if someone really wanted to get rid of a witness, it didn't cost much. Suddenly his role had changed, and he was the witness that was exposed.

Sitting around talking didn't make any sense to Davis. He leaned forward and stared at Boyko. Why not blow the whole thing up? Shut down the casinos. There was so much rot in the industry there was no other way. Waddington knew where the bodies were buried, but getting people to testify, that was another thing.

Davis thought back to the time he was made to testify against his old gang. All the time he spent in hiding. The case took forever to put together. Surely Boyko knew that. And he knew the risk he was taking exposing a key witness. Even if the cops were clean, it only took one person to speak out of turn, say the wrong thing, and the word would be out.

Boyko read his mind. "We can't just blow this whole thing up overnight. We need names, employees, government officials—anyone who's sat back and raked in small fortunes over the years."

Davis noticed he didn't mention cops. They were going about this all wrong. They were getting nowhere, except maybe closer to getting Waddington killed. He stood up suddenly, and all eyes were on him. He turned to Lossan. "I'm sorry," he said. "I can't help anymore. I'm going back east." He ignored Lossan's look, grabbed his jacket from the back of his chair and left the room.

Chapter 29

Doug Waddington sat in the canteen at the lottery corporation. He'd just been called in and reprimanded, told he wasn't a team player and needed to stop being so critical and outspoken about this so-called money laundering at the casinos. He sighed and stared into his coffee mug. He could feel the eyes of the people around him on his back. How could so many people know so much and say so little? It was disheartening, to say the least. He knew his days were numbered.

Had someone found out about his meeting at Langley? No way. That'd be a death sentence.

Waddington picked up his mug and headed to his office. The lights were off. That was puzzling. He never touched the switch until the end of the day. He must be on autopilot. He flicked them on and shut the door behind him. When he turned around, he almost dropped his mug.

Sitting in a chair in the corner near the radiator was the man who'd left the meeting at Tall Timbers yesterday. Davis. The guy who looked more like a gangster than a cop.

"How the hell did you get in the building, let alone my office?"

"Easy," said Davis, flashing a lanyard.

"And the door, I know it was locked."

"Yes, it was. Listen, we don't have a lot of time."

Waddington was at a loss. Something about this guy made him nervous and yet comfortable at the same time. It was a strange sensation. The guy was unpredictable. He gave off a dangerous vibe, but for some reason Waddington felt he could trust him.

"You want to take down the cartel, right? Expose the government guys who've been letting all this happen?"

Waddington nodded. "Yeah, mate. But it's getting a bit late for me. I may be out of here any day."

"I want you to take me to one of the casinos. I need to get the feel of the place.

Waddington surveyed the man for a moment. He'd come here alone. He clearly didn't want anyone to know. He tilted his head. "Do you want to tell me what's going on?"

Davis smiled. "Not yet. For now, let's just say I'm not sure who I can trust, but I'm pretty sure I can trust you."

...

The night air was cold as Davis and Waddington stepped out of the cab and into the River Rock Casino's parking lot. A few people in suits and fancy dresses were laughing and smoking on one side of the entrance. The parking lot was well lit, and Davis and Waddington followed the people heading toward the heavy glass doors.

When they stepped inside, the noise of the outside world began to fade. The place was enormous, bigger than two football pitches. The crimson carpet patterned with gold designs seemed to guide the way to the gaming tables. Davis looked down the hallway and noticed large chandeliers over the room where dealers shuffled cards and players looked both serious and excited.

As they made their way further into the casino, the smell of stale tobacco hit them. They walked past a row of distracting slot machines, the gamblers sitting in front of them were focused on the spinning symbols, most holding a cigarette in one hand and the handle of a slot machine in the other. The waiters and croupiers reeked of smoke.

Davis looked around. One thing was clear. They'd been noticed. It didn't help that they were big guys, but it was more than that. He felt eyes following them through the room as they passed a row of gaming tables, the players staring down at their cards and chips in front of them, some frowning, others keeping a straight face. When they reached a dark wooden door at the end of the room, Davis and Waddington paused for a moment. A security guard dressed in a suit nodded and opened the door.

The private baccarat room beyond was a stark contrast to the bustling casino floor—it was elegant, decorated with dark wood panelling and leather chairs. The smell of smoke was stronger inside. A large, polished table stood in the centre of the room, surrounded by a few high-stakes players seated in plush leather chairs, some leaning heavily over their cards, others looking more relaxed. Davis recognized the smell of expensive cigars. He'd always loved a Cohiba, and at twenty-five bucks a cigar, who wouldn't.

No one looked up when they entered, but Davis knew that one of the dozens of ceiling cameras around the room had caught them by now. He glanced at his companion. Waddington was staring at the table. He turned slightly and motioned with his eyes toward the left.

Davis glanced from the player Waddington had indicated to the two large men on either side of him. They were both staring back. Davis had seen that look plenty of times. These guys were hardcore enforcers. He glanced at the cameras one more time, then motioned to Waddington, and the two of them stepped out of the room.

"I don't know if you've noticed," Davis said, "but we haven't exactly gone under the radar."

Waddington grimaced. "It's the story of my life."

As the door to the baccarat room closed, Davis saw one of the enforcers inside had stood up and was moving toward them. Davis glanced toward the casino and noted two more large men on the move, making it impossible for them to return to the busy floor without being nabbed.

"It was a mistake coming here with you." Davis was angry with himself. He'd suspected someone had tipped off Alarez and the rest of the guys they were chasing. Now he was sure of it. Worse, he and Waddington had just stepped into the middle of things with no protection and nothing to show for their trouble. "We need to get out of here now."

Waddington glanced behind them, down a dimly lit hallway that led to the back of the casino. Other than a few players heading into the men's room, it was deserted. In the other direction, the enforcer from the baccarat room had joined the two from the floor and were walking directly toward them.

"C'mon," Waddington said in a low voice. "We'll go out the back."

Davis looked between Waddington and the men approaching, then turned and began to jog after Waddington, who had already started moving toward the service door at the back of the casino. He could hear footsteps behind them. Waddington pushed through a grey metal door labelled Staff Only. The door swung open with a creak. The dimly lit back parking lot was half empty, cars scattered everywhere. No alarm sounded, but they both knew someone somewhere had just been notified of what they'd done.

The door closed behind them with a soft thud. The footsteps inside had either stopped or were inaudible. Davis glanced around, his eyes adjusting to the low light. The rain was coming down in a depressing drizzle, and shadows cast by the overhead lamps created an eerie atmosphere. "Over here," Davis said.

Waddington followed him to a dumpster, and they ducked down next to it, both realizing they were in trouble if the men decided to follow them into the parking lot.

The door creaked open, and Waddington tried not to move. He hadn't carried a gun in a long time, and he was holding his soft belly to settle his heavy breathing, all the while cursing himself for his lack of exercise. A moment later, the service door closed, and Davis peeked around the side of the dumpster. He stood up cautiously. "Looks like we aren't worth it," he said. "Let's go round to the front."

Davis turned and began to jog along the side of the building with Waddington trying to keep up behind him. Suddenly, the brick next to Davis exploded and a sharp crack echoed through the empty lot— a gunshot. Davis's instincts kicked in. He grabbed Waddington's arm and pulled him down. They stayed low, moving along the cars and finally stopping behind a red Camaro. Davis looking around with glinting eyes. Waddington was heaving, his breath coming in short, panicked bursts.

Behind them, shoes slapped against wet pavement. Another shot rang out, shattering the Camaro's side mirror. "We're dead if we stay here," Davis said. "We have to make a run for it." Waddington nodded, but he didn't like his odds. Neither did Davis. "I'll draw his attention," he said. "When I make my move, you run around to the front of the building and keep going. I'll be right behind you." Davis yanked the broken mirror off the car and shuffled toward the trunk. "Ready?" he whispered.

Waddington nodded. Davis threw the mirror as hard as he could. It smacked the side of a parked car with a clang that echoed across the lot and carried on, skidding across the tarmac toward the opposite side of the lot. The moment he heard the sound, Waddington jumped up and tore in the opposite direction, praying Davis's diversion would be enough. He sprinted toward the front of the casino, his feet slipping slightly on the slick ground. As he rounded the corner, the bright lights of the casino's entrance came into view. Waddington spotted a line of cabs waiting near the entrance, their drivers chatting and smoking, unaware of the chaos unfolding nearby.

With one final burst of energy, he dashed toward the nearest cab, flung the door open and dove inside. The startled cabbie turned around in his seat, a cigarette hanging out of his open mouth. Before he could speak, Davis hurtled toward them and threw himself into the cab next to Waddington.

"Drive! Now!" he shouted.

The driver closed his mouth around his cigarette and slammed his foot down on the gas, speeding away from the casino and the danger behind them.

Inside the darkened cab, Davis's eyes glinted like a cat in the night. "You know the best way to stop us, right?"

Waddington was still gasping for air. Finally he caught his breath. "Get rid of me."

Chapter 30

Slattery was nervous. The ex-cop didn't like being involved with a guy like Alarez, but he had two alimonies and nothing but a shitty apartment to show for his thirty years on the force. He needed the extra cash. It wasn't much, but it made his life a little more bearable. And up to now, he hadn't felt bad about what he was doing. He'd barely told the Mexican anything. And Alarez had told him very little about their operations.

Slattery held his cigarette with yellowed fingers and took a long drag as he looked across the hazy, dimly lit bar. It was more like a biker hangout than a pub. Tables were sticky with old beer and sad memories. Outside, a large neon sign flickered in the misty evening air. God knows why the Mexican had chosen the place. It was next to the Fraser River, and Slattery had trouble finding it because of the fog. He'd barely been able to make out the entrance, and if it wasn't for the neon sign, he'd have missed the place.

A door opened and Slattery stubbed his cigarette out in the ceramic dish on the dirty table. He watched Alarez look left and right as he stepped into the bar. *Like a rat watching for cats*, Slattery thought. Only I'm the rat. He pushed away a few nasty thoughts and nodded at the Mexican as they made eye contact.

Alarez ran a manicured hand over his slick black hair and glanced around again before making his way toward the skinny grey-haired man with the leathery face seated in the corner.

The old cop had been his eyes and ears ever since he'd had to go into hiding. And it barely cost them a thing. The guy was pathetic, but he had friends and was in the know about what went on with both the city police and the drug squad.

Alarez had been told to go underground. Ever since the banker had been taken out, things had started spinning out of control. Now they wanted him to shut down the police investigation. But that wasn't going to be easy.

"What is the update?" Alarez said in a low voice, being careful not to touch the dirty table as he sat down.

Slattery leaned in slightly. "They're still watching your old place. And word is, they suspect you were warned." Alarez's citrusy aftershave lingered between them. It felt out of place in Slattery's world.

Alarez shrugged. They had so many cops in their pocket, what did he care if they suspected someone.

Slattery was looking down. He looked uncomfortable. Like he wasn't happy about something.

Alarez glared at him until the older man met his eyes. "And? What else?" His voice was clipped, clean, like everything about him.

Slattery was sure the Mexican was behind the banker's death. And now he was supposed to tell him about this Waddington guy. There could be only one reason for that.

"I have another name for you," said Slattery finally. At this point, if he didn't do his job, it wasn't about not getting paid. It was about staying alive.

Alarez was getting impatient. "Well?"

"His name's Waddington. He's an ex-cop from Australia. Big guy." Slattery took his cigarette pack and lit up.

"Anything else?"

"You already know the other players. He just said to tell you about Waddington." Slattery took a crumpled paper from his pocket and held it out to Alarez, who looked down at it with disgust. It looked sweaty and there were stains on it. It could have been jam. "It's the Aussie's address."

Alarez snatched the paper with two fingers. "We meet here again in two days. Same time."

Slattery didn't like the word *we*. It made it seem like he was part of whatever Alarez was doing. He preferred to be to the side, the outside.

Alarez pushed through the door and headed into the misty night, his polished shoes clicking across the deserted parking lot. The ex-cop had seemed more nervous than usual. The last thing they needed was for someone to lose their shit and put the operation at risk. Slattery had been useful up to now. Told him about the nosy bean counter who was a friend of the banker and had started all this.

Alarez rounded the corner of the building and headed into the dark alley. He missed his wife and son. He was ready to return home, but the bosses in Sinaloa convinced him he could help more if he stayed. So he stayed. That's one of the reasons he'd risen so quickly within the cartel. The other was his uncle. Teelum Loera was a lead sicario for the cartel. He controlled drug trafficking activities in the city of Guamuchil and supervised over two hundred men. He'd seen something of himself in his nephew. An ambition and drive to get to the top. The boy wasn't afraid to take risks, even as a child of ten.

And his young family guaranteed that he'd always come home and resist the temptation to escape and start a new life in Canada. Vancouver was a beautiful city, and he could have things he never dreamed of in Mexico. But he soon pined for his family and became lonely. He developed contacts within the local Mexican community but was careful. He never got too close to anyone.

Part of him still dreamed of living in Vancouver with his family. If he ever got caught, he thought he might be able to do a deal with the authorities. But how would he get his family to Canada? Unless he progressed up the ranks of the cartel where he'd be able to arrange for vacations for his family abroad. Even then he'd run the risk that they'd track him down. But at least he could dream.

...

The all-night diner was almost empty. Faded photographs and a few trophies from decades before lined a wooden shelf on one side. Along the laminate counter, a couple of truckers were nursing coffees.

Davis hung up the pay phone near the door and headed to the back where Waddington was in a booth near the washrooms. Davis's face was a mask of calm as he slid into his seat, but his eyes betrayed the tension simmering beneath the surface. Waddington was leaning back against the cracked red vinyl. His hands trembled as he reached for the menu.

"Relax," Davis muttered, his voice low and steady. "We're safe here. For now."

"In all my years as a cop, I never got shot at," Waddington said.

Davis had been shot at plenty of times. It never got easier. But they needed to stay focused. "We need to figure out our next move," he said, more to himself.

"Did you talk to Bolton?"

Davis nodded. "He's sending his family out of town. Then he'll meet us."

Chapter 31

Early the next morning, Boyko met with the deputy attorney general to discuss the casino case. He'd decided to hold back some of his evidence. The chances were good that most of the information he revealed would quickly become public information within the AG's office. Doors would quickly close, witnesses might refuse to cooperate and, depending on who was involved, people's lives could be at risk. Experience taught him that laying the groundwork for the appointment of a special prosecutor took time.

"We don't know if public officials participated in a cover-up," Boyko said, "but it looks like some have known about the money laundering for years."

The assistant AG grunted. He cradled his head in his hands as if he felt a migraine coming on. "What will you do if we don't give you access to our records?"

Boyko looked him in the eye. "Your ministry manages the Crown corporation that oversees gaming in the province." He pursed his lips as the man in front of him seemed to visibly pale. "Sir, I don't think you have much choice. And you know it."

...

Lossan had tried to reach Davis earlier that morning, with no luck. He contacted reception and asked if Davis was still staying at the hotel. A pleasant voice confirmed that Mr. Davis was still registered. Lossan left a message asking him to call as soon as possible.

He'd barely hung up the phone when it rang again. It was Cameron. "Charlie Patel's dead," he said.

Lossan couldn't speak for a moment. Then he managed, "What happened?"

"Don't know yet. First cop on the scene told me it looked like a hit. Shot in the back of the head. Found in a dead-end alley just off Cordova, down from Main."

Lossan was staring out his window at nothing, his mind spinning. Was this connected to their operation? Or just bad luck? He knew Holliday would want him down there to find out what went on and what forensics had to say. "Who's in charge?"

"An inspector from Vancouver Police, guy named Callaghan. Don't know him."

Lossan hung up and made a few calls, then he headed downtown.

The crime scene was cordoned off, but when he flashed his badge, the cop controlling the crowd let him through. Lossan walked toward the group at the end of the alley. Three forensic techs in white coveralls surrounded the body. Ten feet away, Haddock was speaking to someone. Lossan guessed it was Inspector Callaghan.

As Lossan approached, Haddock glanced up and nodded, but his focus was on Callaghan.

"From what I can tell," the inspector was saying, "he took a bullet to the back of his head. Of course nobody saw anything around here." He sighed. "I understand Sergeant Patel was no stranger to the Eastside?"

"Worked here for years," said Haddock.

The alley was about thirty yards long, bordered on both sides by six-storey buildings.

"Both buildings have retail on the ground floor and low-rent units above," Callaghan told them. Judging by the area, the rental units were used to house the homeless or people on welfare. "We've checked the retail units," he continued. "There's a passageway that connects all of them to the exit doors leading into the alley. The residential tenants can also access the exit doors. The assailant could've come from just about anywhere."

Lossan asked if they were checking for video footage from the retail stores and whether there were any cameras in the passageways.

"We're running it down as we speak."

Fifteen minutes later, forensics signalled they'd finished, and Patel's body was about to be taken to the morgue. Haddock and Lossan walked down the narrow alley. Haddock's limp seemed worse, Lossan noticed. But if he was in pain, Haddock didn't mention it.

Patel's body lay under a sheet at the end of the alley.

"This is Detective Jones, forensics," Callaghan told them.

Jones nodded at them. "Based on the blood spatter, we think this is where he was murdered. No signs of struggle, though."

Lossan cleared his throat and looked away from the body. "You think he was lured here?"

Jones chewed a big wad of gum as he considered this. "Could be."

Lossan looked around. There were a few dumpsters on either side of the lane, so it was possible someone could have hidden behind one.

The investigator followed Lossan's eyes. "Given the powder burns, he was shot at close range. The angle suggests the shooter was over there. Could've come into the alley through one of those doors." He pointed to four black doors, two on each side of the alley. "There's not much more we can tell you now."

"Time of death?" asked Haddock.

"Late last night, early this morning. A homeless guy called it in." The investigator looked up at the apartments on either side of the alleyway. "It's hard to believe no one heard anything. Mind you, given the tenants, I doubt there'll be any witnesses. We'll check the footage from any cameras inside the retail units and canvass the tenants but..." Jones shrugged.

"Charlie had contact with dealers. This could've been a drug deal gone bad," Haddock said.

Lossan met his eyes and knew the other man was thinking the same thing he was. This wasn't a drug deal gone bad. This had something to do with their investigation.

Chapter 32

It had been a long time since Davis had visited his cabin up north. And winter wasn't the best time to travel. Davis had rented an SUV. He'd had no choice but to give his ID, so he had to hope whoever was looking for them would lose their trail once they got on the road. It was a ten-hour drive from Vancouver. Travelling north on Highway 97 to Williams Lake was bad enough, but the last hundred and fifty miles west was along a two-lane highway that was always covered in snow and often icy at this time of year. There were few towns along the way, and breaking down in the remote wilderness was dangerous. But the cabin was a good place to hide.

Davis glanced in the rearview mirror at Bolton. He still looked shell-shocked. He'd picked up his messages before they left town and told the group about Charlie Patel's murder. The tension in the car was palpable, though Davis was good at hiding his feelings. The shooting at the casino had rattled him too. The enemy was closing in and they didn't have much time...

Davis tried to focus on the way ahead. His old friend Roy Long Feathers had died years back, but his son Henry was still there, and he'd promised to keep an eye on the place until Davis returned. Like his father, Henry asked no questions and left him alone. He was still living in his dad's old house on the Ulkatcho First Nation reserve.

"Davis," Bolton said from the back, "the more I think about it, the more I'm convinced this is bloody mad. You must tell Lossan where—"

"In case you haven't figured it out, I trust no one, especially cops." Davis glared at him in the rearview mirror.

"And Patel has just been murdered," Waddington said darkly.

"We don't know for sure that's connected," Bolton said.

Davis shook his head. "I've dealt with too many crooked cops in my time. I'm not saying any guys on Lossan's team are crooked, but they deal with cops that are. I mean on the street. All these guys have been working the streets for years. They become cynical. What have they got to look forward to? A pension and that's it. No villa in Mexico or condo in Hawaii."

"But you trust Lossan, yes?" Bolton asked.

Davis pursed his lips. "Can't say why, but yeah, I do. But Lossan trusts everyone, so if we tell him where we're going, he'll feel obligated to share it with the group." Davis narrowed his eyes. "You did tell Lossan you were heading out of town with your family, right?"

Bolton nodded. He didn't like lying to his friend, but when all this was over, he'd make it up to him somehow. He stared out the window. They were already out of the city. Trees were flashing by, and the farther they got from Vancouver, the farther they were from the danger. So why didn't he feel safer? Maybe it was the thought of a cabin in the middle of nowhere. If they were found, they'd be all alone. He didn't have a gun. And he wouldn't know what to do with one even if he did.

Davis was thinking about how long they might have to be in hiding. The special prosecutor route would take forever. They weren't getting any closer to finding Alarez, and he doubted whoever was behind the attack at the casino had given up. Sooner or later someone would track them down, especially since it was clear there was a leak. In hindsight, it might have been better if Waddington had flown back to Australia. But they'd track him down there. At least here, Davis felt like he was controlling things.

He looked out at the highway traffic headed back into the city and then checked his rearview mirror again. "I've been meaning to tell you something, Waddington."

Waddington turned and looked out the rear window. "You think we're being followed?"

"No, we're not being followed. But you know I'm not a cop, don't you?"

"What're you on about?"

"I do undercover work for the cops, but … I'm not a cop. I should have told you before now, but there was never an opportunity."

Bolton braced himself. He thought they might be turning around very soon.

"I'm an ex-con. Did time. Went into witness protection years ago, then went undercover in Montreal. Don't worry. Lossan, Boyko and the other cops all know about my background. Lossan's the guy that arrested me years ago in Vancouver, and Boy Scout in the back there, well, he helped Lossan get me arrested. It's a long story, but I thought you needed to know, especially since were going to be spending some time together up north."

Waddington was silent for a full minute. Then he said, "You mean to tell me the cops hired an ex-con to help in this operation and I'm the last one to know…"

"Yeah, yeah," said Davis, "but we didn't know you'd be part of the team."

Waddington seemed to be thinking about this. "It's funny," he said finally.

"What is?"

"This is the first time I've seen you stressed."

"I thought you'd be furious."

"Well, I would've been, but Lossan told me about your background the first day we met." Waddington let out a crack of laughter.

Davis smiled. The guy had a sense of humour.

Bolton leaned over the seats between them. "He had you going, didn't he?"

"Did you know he knew?" Davis asked.

"Of course not. But he had you worried, didn't he?"

Waddington laughed. "Your face was a picture. Lossan told me the whole story. Even how Boyko's guys called Montreal to check you out. I gather you're quite the hero."

Davis shrugged. "I wouldn't go that far."

They were quiet for a few minutes, until Waddington turned in his seat and said brightly, "Well, that's it then, isn't it? We might as well accept things as they come, fellas. We're stuck together. And for a while from the sounds of things."

...

Lossan tried Davis's hotel again that afternoon. He was wondering if Davis really had gone back to Miramichi. He thought he'd been bluffing.

"Mr. Davis ... ummm, oh yes, nice gentleman. Said he was headed back east. Said he was thinking of doing some fishing. I was surprised when he said it, sir. I didn't know you could fish in the winter. We had a little chat about it. I know nothing about fishing, sir, but Mr. Davis sounds like quite the angler."

Lossan remembered Davis used to be a fishing guide back in Miramichi. He frowned. Damn him, the guy had really left. He always knew this operation was a long shot. But with Davis gone, it felt hopeless. Maybe the whole thing never had a chance.

Chapter 33

The drive to Williams Lake was uneventful. There wasn't much snow on the road, but Davis knew the hard part would be the last three and a half hours west to Anahim Lake. It was getting dark and he needed a break. Bolton and the Australian had offered to drive, but Davis knew the road, even though it'd been years since he'd driven it. They'd stop for dinner and, with luck, be at the cabin by ten. Davis remembered the times he'd driven to the cabin before and how he'd felt after leaving the city behind. It was as if the weight of the world had been lifted. Back then he'd been driving away from his own problems.

He always liked the beautiful wide-open wilderness, the fact that there weren't many people and the peace and quiet. That's what he'd liked about Miramichi. Maybe he could live in BC after all, if he spent time up north. He could never settle in Vancouver. Too much traffic, too many people, everyone in a rush to get somewhere—and it rained forever.

They found a small restaurant on the outskirts of Williams Lake. The town was always a bottleneck. The rail line went right through the middle, and you could almost guarantee a cargo train with more than a hundred railcars would be on the tracks, holding up the traffic.

Bolton was already missing his family. "You think we might be stuck up here in the middle of nowhere for months?" he said to nobody in particular.

Waddington heard the sadness in the other man's voice. "I'm sure it won't be too long. I can't hide up here indefinitely."

"You'll be safe," Davis said. "That's what matters. Once we know where this is going, we can make more permanent plans. I put myself in their place and think about what I'd do if I were them. I like to be one step ahead."

"Who exactly are we talking about?" asked Bolton. "I mean, this is the cartel, right? You don't suppose someone who works for the casinos…"

Davis raised an eyebrow. "Could be the cartel, the triads, someone involved in the casinos." He looked between them. "Maybe even a cop."

Bolton leaned forward and ate his soup. How had he gotten here? From comforting his dead friend's wife to hiding out with an ex-con. It all seemed surreal. He could have gone into hiding with his family. Davis had offered that. But he'd also told him he thought he was valuable. That his being trustworthy and invested was important for the investigation. It was unusual for Davis to show a caring side, and even more unusual for him to tell someone they were valuable. Maybe even Davis was getting desperate and wanted all the help he could get.

But they were finally getting somewhere with Waddington's evidence. And it had been a long time since Bolton had felt like he was really making a difference. There was always a demand for forensic investigators. But no one called you a hero for doing it. Bolton grimaced. He'd always put on the cape as a kid. Helping people gave him the dopamine he needed. But now that he was here and his family was far away, he felt a bit foolish.

They finished their dinner quickly. Despite being tired, Davis was anxious to get back on the road. There were fewer and fewer cars out this way. A little over three hours later, they'd left the one-lane highway and were the only ones on the tiny snow-covered dirt road.

Davis slowed down and was grateful for the four-wheel drive on the SUV he'd rented. The road had been plowed sometime in the last few days, so it was passable, but most of the unlit lanes to people's cabins were blocked with snow drifts. Ten minutes later, when they turned onto the lane to his place, he was glad he'd thought to call Henry ahead of time. It was freshly plowed, and the lights were on in the old log cabin.

Waddington woke up slowly in the front seat and looked around. From the back, Bolton grew anxious when someone appeared at the door, but Davis waved from the front seat. Then he pulled a flashlight from between the seats, got out and stretched. He shone the light toward the old barn. Henry had already turned on the small generator, and there were other things in there he'd check on later. He opened the back of the SUV and pulled out Waddington's carry-on. They hadn't risked going back to his place before leaving, so they'd hit a local second-hand store. Davis bought a few things for himself and then a new toothbrush at drugstore on the way out of town. What more did he need?

Davis walked over to the porch. Behind him Bolton and Waddington were lugging their bags across the slippery driveway.

The guy at the door gave Davis a bear hug. He was four inches taller than Davis and had long hair. "Alan, it's been a long time. How are you?"

"Tired. I'm getting old." They tromped into the small mudroom and wiped their feet. "Henry, this is Paul and Doug. They'll be staying here for a while."

"Of course. Come on, let's get your bags in." Henry took Bolton's bag into the larger living area beyond. "I put the fire on a few hours ago and got some groceries in," he called over his shoulder as Waddington removed his shoes. There'd been no winter boots for him at the second-hand store.

Davis nodded toward a closet. "I've got some extra gear in there. You might find something that fits you." He followed Henry into the main room. "You haven't told anyone I was coming up here, have you?"

Henry looked over his shoulder to make sure the others couldn't hear them and whispered, "You told me not to. Even my wife doesn't know. Tomorrow I'll pick up those special items you ordered from Williams Lake."

Davis nodded and looked around. It had been years since he'd been to the cabin, but every time he came up here, he felt like he'd just left the day before. Henry had taken good care of the place. It was clean, dusted, tidy and neat. A fire blazed in the fireplace and welcomed them.

Davis turned to the two men he'd driven up with. "If we keep to the cabin, there's a good chance no one will know we're here. The locals are very friendly, but they want to know everyone's business." He looked out the window where snow was now falling.

"I can get anything you need from the store," Henry offered.

Davis smiled at his old friend. "How many officers are at the RCMP detachment these days?"

"They're down to five now." Henry put the coffee pot back on the Aga to heat it up.

Davis looked at Waddington and Bolton. "There are two rooms in the back. I'll sleep in the armchair. Unless the barn is ready, Henry?"

"Still a bit cold in there. Should be fine for tomorrow evening though."

Chapter 34

Sam Coyle had been a journalist with the *Vancouver Sun* for almost fifteen years and covered both provincial and federal politics. He'd had a few scoops in his time and developed a reputation for getting to the bottom of a story. The thick package that landed on his desk was marked private and confidential. It had been hand delivered that morning and his name was typed in bold letters. As he opened it, he found a copy of a document signed by the province's deputy attorney general. It was the appointment of a special prosecutor.

Coyle laid the contents of the envelope out on his desk and began scanning the documents. The words *money laundering* and *BC Casinos* jumped out at him. Then the names of two mid-level government deputy minsters. He rifled through the pages, his heart hammering. There was an affidavit sworn by a senior officer in the RCMP, an eight-page report of RCMP findings and a copy of a report entitled "Project Clean-Up."

Coyle looked around the newsroom. Most of the desks were occupied by other reporters. Many were talking on the phone. Others were tapping away on their Macs. He'd got used to the white noise in the background and could work anywhere. But this was different. He needed a quiet place and privacy. One of his buddies looked at him. "What you got there, Sammy?"

He quickly gathered up all the documents and stacked them in a pile. "Not sure yet. I need to make a call."

"Another hot story? Need help?"

"Nah, just some city council story I've been following up on. You know, the usual." He pretended to look at his watch, then stood up and put the documents in his briefcase. "Got to go."

When he got back to his apartment, Coyle laid the documents across his desk and slowly read each page. Two hours later, he sat back, stretched and took a swig of cold coffee. He grimaced and set the mug down. He'd gotten through all the documents and couldn't believe what he'd read. He'd heard rumours but he'd never been able to put the pieces together. His boss would want proof. Some third-party confirmation. He needed help from someone in the paper, maybe a crime reporter. He thought of Nolan. She'd developed a reputation—tough, fearless, wouldn't back down, even though her life had been threatened several times by organized crime.

Why had they sent the package to him? Most of his stories were about politics, not crime. Maybe that was the point—this had wider implications. Nolan had contacts; she was also someone who'd be happy to share the credit and knew which buttons to press.

When he phoned and told her he needed to meet, she said she was busy and could meet in a few days. He told her it couldn't wait.

There was a moment of silence. "What's so urgent, Sammy?"

"Trust me you won't regret it, but we have to meet in person."

...

That night at eight o'clock, Coyle headed into a small bar in New Westminster. The place was full. Sara Nolan was seated in a booth in the corner all on her own, nursing a glass of cider. Nolan was barely five feet tall, but she wasn't scared of anyone. She deserved her reputation as a ruthless investigative crime reporter, unafraid to print the truth. She'd gone after Hells Angels, drug traffickers and fraudsters that preyed on old people. She didn't back down and would argue with cops, politicians and anyone she believed was wrong or was covering something up. She also knew how to handle the editor and the lawyers who vetted the contentious stories that could get the newspaper in trouble. She'd even threatened to quit when they refused to publish one of her stories. Sammy was pretty sure he'd picked the right person to help get the story out.

Nolan raised her eyebrows when Sammy approached her. "This better be worth my time."

Sammy opened his satchel and pulled out a wad of documents. "Take a look at this." He handed over the documents.

She skimmed the first page, flipped quickly through a few more, then looked up at him. "Where did you get this?"

"Anonymous drop-off at the newsroom."

Nolan flicked from page to page. A few times, she opened her mouth as if to say something. *She's hooked*, thought Sammy. "What are you drinking?"

"Cider."

He headed to the bar. When he returned, she looked up at him. "Jesus, I can't believe it. Have you read all this?"

"Every word."

"I heard rumours, but this, this is dynamite. You know what this means if it's true?" Her eyes were glowing. "I need time to take this all in. I can't do it here. Listen, I live two blocks away. I'd like to read it at home."

"Fine, but I'm coming too."

"One thing. Why did they send this to you?"

"I asked myself the same question. The only thing I can think of is the government angle. This isn't just about crime. It's about who's involved, who knew and what they knew. And was there a cover-up…"

"Mmm. Probably a frustrated cop sent it," said Nolan. "Someone who doesn't believe this will go anywhere unless it's made public." She shook her head, her eyes once again focused on the papers. "Can you imagine if this gets out?"

"You mean *when*."

She smiled at that and stood up. She barely reached his shoulder. "Come on, let's go. This is going to take a while. We can grab some pizza on the way back to my place."

She scooped up the documents before he could and was halfway to the door before he began to move.

...

It was close to midnight by the time Nolan had finished reading the documents for the third time. She'd been making notes on a pad as she went and kept going back to her notes and underlining passages. To kill time, Sammy reread each document after she'd finished it. A few things he wasn't quite sure about before became much clearer.

Nolan took off her glasses and rubbed her eyes.

"What do you think?" Sammy asked.

"We need a way to prove this is all true," she said. "I have some contacts in the force, but we need to tread carefully. They'll close ranks." She looked at him thoughtfully. "We need to get the whole story out, not just the fact that a special prosecutor's been appointed. The money laundering, the triads, the cartel ... and the national security angle. You sure you have no idea who gave this to you?"

He'd been thinking about that too. "It wasn't couriered to the paper; some kid just dropped it off."

Nolan smiled. "Someone wanted to remain anonymous. But does it really matter? All we need to do is make sure it's real."

Chapter 35

Davis didn't get much sleep that night. The armchair he was in must have been forty years old. It was still dark when he got up and made himself a coffee. He wanted to take a shower but worried that he might wake up his guests. He took his coffee to the front porch of the cabin and settled on the bench next to the woodpile. His old axe was leaning next to it. It was bitterly cold, probably minus fifteen, and he headed back inside to the kitchen. Henry had bought the basics, but Davis didn't feel like cooking. He remembered the local restaurant opened early. Forestry personnel and construction contractors often ate there before going to work.

Davis pulled a woollen hat with earflaps over his head and threw on a heavy old coat with a collar that covered half his face. He felt confident no one would look twice at him. Before leaving, he scrawled a quick message and dropped it on the kitchen table, then grabbed his keys. He turned right onto Highway 20 and pulled into the gravel motel parking lot less than ten minutes later. The lights in the restaurant were on, but the door was locked. He knocked and a middle-aged women opened the door.

"Any chance of breakfast?"

"We don't open till six thirty, love, but I can make you coffee. Cook will be here anytime."

Davis looked at his watch. Six twenty. He was always an early riser and loved this time of the day. Mostly because there weren't too many people around. He grabbed a booth near the door. Even the restaurant was cold. He kept his coat and hat on.

"You're up early, love," said the waitress as she poured him coffee. He must have looked a sight. He hadn't shaved, hadn't even changed his clothes. She probably took him for a contractor from one of the camps. He'd heard there were infrastructure projects on the go in the area. A new bridge was being built in the valley and road construction was always taking place. He wondered whether the road to Bella Coola had been improved. It must have been over twenty years since he'd driven it with George Koehle. He chuckled at the memory. Poor old George had thought he was going to die on that hill. Davis wondered where he was now.

He looked at the menu, which reminded him how hungry he was. He swore it hadn't changed since he was last here. They still had the ham-and-cheese omelette. Davis felt the years melt away as he waited for his food. The area brought back memories. Good memories. The wide-open wilderness, fishing, hunting, fresh air, beautiful lakes and peace and quiet. Maybe he'd come back in the spring—if he was still in Vancouver. *Who knows*, he thought, *maybe I could stay for a while.* He'd fix the cabin up. He'd always intended to renovate. Or maybe he'd build a new one. He remembered driving by a couple of log home manufacturers in Williams Lake years ago. He liked the look of the units in their yard. He figured labour and materials would be cheap. He didn't need anything fancy.

He polished off the omelette, hashbrowns and toast in no time. He had another coffee. But it wasn't enough to keep him awake, because the next thing he knew, the waitress was rubbing his shoulder. "Wake up, love. Maybe you should go back to bed."

Davis rubbed his eyes. "Sorry, I had a long drive yesterday and didn't get much sleep when I got in."

"Here, take this." She gave him a coffee in a to-go cup. "You be careful. I don't want you falling asleep at the wheel."

Davis thanked her and left the restaurant.

By the time he was back at the cabin, Bolton and Waddington were up and dressed.

"You both look like you slept okay."

Bolton was the first to speak. "I did. It's so quiet up here."

"Same for me," said Waddington. "How about you? That armchair doesn't look very comfortable."

Davis nodded toward the bottle of blended whisky still sitting on the small bookshelf next to the chair. "I had some help," he said. He motioned toward the kitchen area. "Henry's got bread. The toaster's there. Or you can cook eggs if you feel like it. I see you've made some coffee."

He headed to the small bathroom, showered and went to his bedroom. Waddington's clothes from the day before were on the chair in the corner. Davis took a minute to find some old clean clothes, still in his dresser, and got dressed. He sat on the bed to put on his socks, then he stayed there a moment and picked up the framed photo of his ex-wife and daughter. That was a long time ago. He put it down again and lay on the bed. The pine boards on the ceiling were comforting. He closed his eyes.

They came in the middle of the night. There must have been a dozen of them. In trucks, on foot. They parked across the gravel lane, thirty yards from the road, blocking vehicles from entering or leaving the property.

Davis lay on the ground using the fallen log to set up his high-powered rifle. He aimed at one oil tank, then another, then another. The explosions could be heard miles away. He knew it would take just seconds for the fire to spread to the house. He wasn't disappointed. The others waited in the trees for the occupants to rush out of the cabin. One by one they were gunned down.

Davis woke up from his dream. He was covered in sweat. Was this how it would end?

Chapter 36

Patel's murder was a priority for the Vancouver police. Within a few days they'd interviewed the staff from the retail units backing onto the alley, but the tenants in the rental buildings were harder to track down. Many were addicts or dealers or people suffering from various mental disorders. One of the cops said most of the residents were so strung out, they wouldn't have noticed if someone was standing right in front of them with a gun. It wasn't that they had no suspects, there was just too many to choose from.

Lossan realized that their best intel would likely be word on the street from gang members on the Eastside. Sooner or later they'd get a name. It was thought that Patel may have been executed by a Vietnamese gang. Rumours were circulating that rival gangs were in a turf war. Had he just been in the wrong place at the wrong time? Unlikely, based on the execution-style murder. So was his cover blown? Was an informant involved?

All these thoughts were swirling through Lossan's mind as he walked down the hall and stepped into his boss's office for a morning meeting. Holliday listened as the corporal confided his worries.

"You think it's connected?" said Holliday.

"Nothing concrete," Lossan admitted. "It's just Patel was known to be careful, worked downtown for years—and now this. Sure he had lots of drug contacts, but I don't think it was a deal gone wrong, that'd be a knife in the gut. He was shot in the back of the head."

Holliday didn't like this at all. "Whether its connected or not, we need to be careful. If someone knows about our operation, they'll be trying to put a stop to things."

"That means we're all targets," Lossan said.

Holliday nodded. "Until we can prove otherwise, we must assume Patel's death was related to the operation. Anyone connected is at risk."

...

The following week, Lossan arrived at his office and found a copy of the *Vancouver Sun* on his desk with a handwritten sticky note on the front page. *Looks like someone wanted to make sure your investigation wasn't stalled.*

Lossan set down his keys and picked up the paper. The front-page headline said that a special prosecutor had been hired to investigate claims that organized crime was laundering hundreds of millions of dollars through BC casinos, that casino operators were involved and that some government employees were aware of everything and doing nothing about it.

Lossan dropped into his seat. The paper promised a five-part series over the next few weeks, including an exposé on drug trafficking in Vancouver and the transportation of weapons, counterfeit products and stolen cars. The follow-up stories would show how the proceeds from crime in Vancouver were used to finance more drug trafficking and terrorist activities in other parts of the world.

Lossan didn't know how to feel. Someone had betrayed their operation. But was that really a bad thing? Now that it was all out there and people were starting to ask questions, he felt as if their investigation couldn't be derailed.

A knock at the door interrupted his thoughts. Cameron poked his head into the room.

Lossan held up the paper.

"Ah, you saw it," Cameron said. "Now we can take some real action."

Lossan eyed Cameron suspiciously. Why had he visited him at Heather Street? Why not just phone? "Who do you think leaked the story?"

"I'd like to think it was a cop in the know. But I doubt it," said Cameron.

"Why? Who else would know?"

"Boyko's been trying to get a special prosecutor appointed for weeks. He's been leaning on everyone he knows. Word gets around."

Lossan nodded. All this time, he thought their small task force could keep a secret.

"You can guarantee the politicians will deny any knowledge or involvement and run for the hills," Cameron said. "But what do I know about BC politics?" He shrugged. "Anyway, I'd say it's a win for us. Can't do anything but help."

Lossan set the paper aside and leaned back in his chair. "Any other developments?"

"The streets are quieter than usual lately," Cameron told him. "Instead of the chaos Davis was hoping for, it's like they're all keeping their heads down. No one wants to talk—about cartel connections or Patel's murder." Cameron sighed. "And you should know, Boyko isn't convinced... He thinks it could just be a drug deal gone bad."

Lossan frowned. He couldn't pin it down, but that explanation didn't sit right. He wished he could talk to Davis. But he realized it didn't matter. Of course Davis would say Patel's murder was related to their operation.

"Have you spoken to Davis or Waddington lately?" he asked Cameron.

"Not since our last meeting. Didn't Davis say he was going back east?"

"Yeah, but I don't think he did. It's just a feeling. And I can't get hold of Waddington. His secretary said he had a family emergency and flew back to Australia. We checked the airlines and can't find any evidence that he's taken a flight. And there's something else. I've been looking into any odd goings-on over the past few days. There was a 911 call a few nights ago. Someone reported hearing what they thought was gunfire outside River Rock Casino."

"From what Waddington says, that's not unusual. You think this has something to do with Waddington and Davis?" Cameron asked.

Lossan shrugged. "It's a long shot, but I'm going to head over there today and see if I can have a look at their security footage. At least we'll see if they were there that evening."

"You think they're just going to let you look at their footage?"

Lossan sighed. Cameron was right. And he'd never get a warrant. "Maybe someone will talk to me. Davis isn't the type of guy you'd forget. Maybe someone saw something."

"I'll put some feelers out for you. But if they are both gone, it could mean something else. It's clear Davis doesn't trust cops. Maybe he thought Waddington would be safer out of the way."

The thought had crossed Lossan's mind. And then he remembered George Koehle. And the cabin up north. Where was that again?

"Thanks, Cameron," he said distractedly. "I'll let you know if I track them down." Cameron left. Had Lossan already said too much? That's when he decided that if he did find out where they were, he wouldn't be in a hurry to tell Cameron or anyone else.

Something didn't sit right. Why did Cameron stop by? And he could have found a way to check the video footage, but didn't offer to help. Lossan shook his head. Davis was right. What was it he said years ago? *Only the paranoid survive.* No wonder the guy was always on edge.

Lossan drove home at five o'clock. When he pulled into his driveway, he realized he didn't know how he'd gotten there. He'd been completely distracted by Patel's murder and Davis and Waddington disappearing. When he got out of his car, he didn't go in the house, despite the cold. He took a few deep breaths and walked around his small front yard. The flowers needed deadheading, and he should have gotten the bird feeders up by now.

Then it came to him, as things often did when he let his mind slip. He remembered where Davis's cabin was located, west of Williams Lake near Tweedsmuir Provincial Park, not far from Anahim Lake.

...

Slattery was asleep in his La-Z-Boy when the phone rang. Reluctantly, he opened his eyes. The damn thing was out of reach. He pulled the handle on the side of his chair and heaved himself up, almost knocking over one of the empty beer bottles on the table next to him.

"Yeah." He hiked up his pants as he waited.

"Something's happened."

It was Alarez. Slattery gritted his teeth. He didn't like the way things had been going. He needed out of this. "I know. I read the paper. A cop was murdered."

"I'm talking about the newspaper article. The one about the investigation, the special prosecutor. My friends in Sinaloa are not happy. This makes things ... difficult for us."

Slattery hadn't seen that story. Truth is, he'd been on a bit of a bender. It started after he'd heard about Patel's murder. He hadn't wanted to hear anymore after that.

"They think a cop leaked the story," Alarez said. "Or maybe an ex-cop who does not want to keep doing work for us."

Slattery glanced around as though Alarez might pop out from behind the couch. "I wouldn't—I didn't say anything."

Alarez knew Slattery wasn't the leak. He just liked scaring the guy. Keeping him on his toes. Growing up, all Alarez knew was violence and intimidation. He'd witnessed his uncle shooting two men in the head just because he needed to send a message. At the time, his uncle had told him that the only way to maintain power was through fear and intimidation.

"If we find out that you did, you know what will happen?"

Slattery just stood there dumbly. He was still half drunk. Lately, he couldn't sleep unless he passed out. He'd given up on beer and switched to rum. One of his exes had a thing for strawberry daquiris, and he found a bottle of Bacardi almost full in the back of his cupboard.

"Did you get what I asked for?" Alarez was saying.

Slattery looked around the room. It was a mess. Old takeout containers with half-rotted food remnants were on the living room table amid beer bottles and the now-empty rum bottle. Slattery shuffled over to his kitchen table and picked up a file. "Yeah, I got it," he said, flipping open the folder and dropping the paper inside onto the floor. He groaned as he leaned over to pick it up.

"Are you drunk?"

"What? No, no. I just dropped—never mind. I have the info you wanted." Slattery blinked a few times and held the paper away from his face so it was less blurry. "Uh, Doug Waddington rents a property in downtown Vancouver. He's single. Two siblings and both parents still alive and living back in Melbourne, Australia. Alan Davis lives in Miri … Miramichi, back east, but he's been staying at the Executive Inn in North Burnaby. Has an ex-wife in Burnaby and a daughter in Coquitlam. And he owns a five-acre piece of land up in the Caribou, fifteen miles from Anahim Lake."

"So he might be staying with his wife or more likely, his daughter."

Slattery frowned. What had he just done? "Nah. He'd never put them in danger."

"Give me the addresses."

Slattery closed his eyes for a moment.

"Slattery." Alarez had a way of commanding without raising his voice. It was unnerving. The ex-cop sank into a kitchen chair and instinctively looked around for a drink.

"The addresses."

"Yeah," Slattery said. He blinked a few times, then picked up the paper with the directions to Davis's cabin and the addresses of Davis's ex-wife and daughter. He read it out to Alarez.

"Now you go to this cabin," Alarez said. "See if they are there and then report back to me."

Slattery dropped the paper again and rubbed one eye with his free hand. "Go … where?"

"Tonight, Slattery."

It was well past midnight, and Slattery was in no condition to drive. But there was no point in protesting. Alarez had already hung up.

…

Slattery found a room at a motel in Anahim Lake. He was exhausted after driving all night. He'd grabbed some lunch at the motel restaurant, but the idea of chasing down Davis made him feel sick. He unlocked his room and threw his bag on the chair in the corner. The phone on the bedside table reminded him he was supposed to check in with Alarez, but that meant he'd have to investigate Davis's property, and he could barely keep his eyes open. He'd just sleep for an hour or two. Then he'd go see this goddam cabin and call Alarez with the information. He collapsed on the bed and was snoring in seconds.

Chapter 37

Alarez threw another gun into his bag. Slattery should have checked in yesterday. That meant the drunk was either passed out or dead. *Or he's going to be soon*, Alarez thought darkly. He had two guys watching Davis's wife and daughter. They'd reported no sign of anything unusual, so he was pretty sure Davis and the others were up at his property in the middle of nowhere.

Alarez threw a few more clothes in his bag and hesitated. He picked up a picture of his wife and son and stared at it for a moment. He had to finish the job. It might not stop the investigation, but no one would be able to deny he had done his part. Taking out the key witness would earn him some cred. And maybe save his family from … he dropped the photo on his bed. This was no time for weakness.

Alarez grabbed his bag and the keys of the rental vehicle and headed out the door. He sat in the front seat of the black Ford Explorer and spread out the map he'd picked up at the gas station. It was a ten-hour drive. The three guys he'd be picking up could take the wheel for most of it. Alarez wanted to be alert when he got there. He started the engine and headed to their meeting place. On the drive, he thought about whether he should dump the vehicle and guns once they'd finished the job and fly back to Vancouver. Once the cops found the bodies, they'd be all over the place. He wasn't worried about the local RCMP detachment, he could deal with them. But hanging around for a late-afternoon flight was risky, and the cops would probably be checking the roads. It'd be easy to check the small airport in Bella Coola, and flights would be unreliable that time of year. He'd read there was often fog. Williams Lake airport also had problems with weather at that time of year. No, flying out of a small airport anywhere up north would be a mistake.

He decided they'd drive to Williams Lake and split up once they'd finished the job. Then they'd have options. Some could drive south to Vancouver or north and east to Alberta. But they couldn't hang around. It wouldn't be tough to set up roadblocks in any of these small northern towns.

He pulled into a narrow driveway and hit the horn. A moment later, three guys with bags like his came out the front door of a rundown house. One of them opened the garage and pulled out a large black hockey bag. Alarez assumed it was full of weapons.

Alarez slid out of the driver's seat, opened the trunk and handed the keys to one of them, then climbed into the passenger seat. The guys threw their gear in the back and got in.

"Let's go," Alarez said. If this bastard Waddington was at the cabin, he'd be taken out. If Davis was there, it'd be a bonus. He'd deal with Slattery later.

Chapter 38

Waddington had never been bothered by the rain in Vancouver, but he hated cold weather. He'd gone out to try chopping some firewood for exercise. But it was so damn cold, and the ground was so hard. He was back in the cabin in less than a minute.

He was a city person at heart, and he missed the people and the home comforts. No phone, no television, not even a radio. There were a few books in the cabin, but they were all old, and his tastes didn't stretch to philosophy, First Nations history, yoga or nature. And there was no way he was going to try the yoga poses he found in one of them. It gave him a different picture of Davis.

Bolton, on the other hand, seemed energized by the location. He came from his bedroom and dropped the crime novel he'd brought with him on the small wooden table in the kitchen. "I'm off to the barn. Davis is already there. Care to join?"

Waddington glanced out the window and shivered. Fat snowflakes were dropping onto the frozen porch. "I think I'll make some more coffee," he said.

Bolton pulled on his boots and coat and headed out into the white silence. As he left, he nodded to Davis's friend Henry, who came in the door with a shotgun in one hand and a paper bag filled with groceries in the other. He set the gun down next to the door, wiped his feet and carried the bag to the kitchen counter.

"Just a few more things," he said kindly. "Thought you might like some steak tonight."

Waddington wondered if he meant Caribou or real steak. He helped put the groceries away and made coffee for the two of them. Henry took out a pack of Oreos and tore it open and dumped a few on a plate.

"You ever play cribbage?" Henry asked.

Waddington was delighted.

"There's a board around here somewhere." Henry found it on the bookshelf with a deck of playing cards stacked on top. He brought them over and the men sat with their coffees and Oreos.

As Waddington shuffled the deck, he looked thoughtfully at Henry. This man probably hadn't seen Davis in years, yet here he was, helping them, keeping them company. And the little cabin was clean with lots of firewood.

"How well do you know Davis?" he asked.

"Since I was born," Henry answered. "My father and he were good friends. Alan is a good man; he looks out for people. Up here we don't ask too many questions. I know my dad had a lot of time for him. He used to say there's good in everyone."

Waddington dealt six cards each and the two men sat quietly for a few moments, pondering their next move. "So you know about his past?" Waddington asked.

"Sure. I knew he'd been in trouble with the police, used to be in some gang. Dad knew he was running from something. But he didn't care. Said Alan was never happier than when he was up here. Years ago he brought another fella up here. Same as you. He was trying to hide the guy. Alan was afraid of something or someone."

Waddington tossed two cards face down on the table. Henry added his two to the crib, then said, "Do you want to tell me what you're hiding from?"

"Didn't Davis tell you?"

"No." Henry cut the deck and flipped up the start card, then frowned when he saw it.

Waddington grinned. That boded well for him. "We're not

actually sure who's after us," he admitted. "There's some trouble that involves … well quite a few bad actors. Could be triads, a drug cartel, people that have a lot at stake financially."

"Triads?"

"Chinese organized crime. They've set up shop in Vancouver. They've been using our casinos to launder their money for some time now. But no one's doing anything about it." Waddington realized he'd raised his voice. He took an Oreo and sank back into his chair.

Henry was watching him. "You must know a lot if they're after you."

Waddington nodded. "I used to be a cop."

Henry looked surprised. He accidentally glanced down at Waddington's soft belly.

Waddington chuckled. "Not for several years. But I worked a lot of cases back in Oz. Never thought I'd be on this end of things. That I'd be a sitting target."

"Alan is smart," Henry said. "If there was anyone in the world I'd want to be with if I was in your position, it'd be Alan."

…

In the small barn on the side of the driveway, Davis had unlocked a large chest and was bent over, looking inside when Bolton came in. Davis turned and Bolton stepped back, a little surprised. The ex-gangster was holding a high-powered rifle. Davis smiled and motioned for Bolton to look inside.

The chest was filled with weapons. There were rifles, shotguns and several handguns. There were also a few hunting knives and who knew what else at the bottom of the chest. Grenades? A rocket launcher?

"Well," Bolton said, "I suppose you have enough weapons." What he was thinking was, *I'm hiding out with bloody Rambo.*

Davis smiled at him. "Just in case the cartel comes knocking."

Bolton didn't smile back. "Do you honestly think they'll find us way up here?" It felt impossible. Bolton had never been so off the grid.

"They may have already," Davis said. He softened his tone a bit when he saw Bolton's face. "Henry just told me there's a stranger in town. And he didn't like the look of him."

"And you reckon…"

Davis shrugged. "I think we don't take any chances." Davis tucked a handgun into the back of his pants and shut the lid of the chest. "Henry got me the guy's licence plate. I'm gonna go to town to check things out."

"You're leaving us?" Bolton's eyes were wide.

"Henry's gonna stay until I'm back." Davis put a hand on Bolton's shoulder. "Don't worry, he knows how to use a shotgun better than I do."

...

Lossan was relieved when he heard Davis's voice on the other end of the line. And a little angry. He didn't like being left out of the loop.

"Couldn't risk it," Davis explained. He didn't sound sorry. "Waddington took me to the River Rock, and we got run outta there. Someone took a few shots at us in the back parking lot."

"I'm aware," Lossan said.

"You are? How did you know?"

"I'm a corporal with the RCMP for god's sake." Lossan couldn't help adding, "I knew you'd pull something like this. When you disappeared, I checked into recent 911 calls. It led me to the River Rock. There were reports of shots fired. Some cabbie claimed two guys scared the hell out of him when they jumped into his vehicle and demanded they be dropped on the side of the road in the middle of nowhere. I figured it must have been you."

"I'm impressed," Davis said.

Lossan wasn't finished. "And I haven't forgotten about your cabin, Davis."

"I'm more impressed."

Lossan was slightly mollified. At least he hadn't headed back to the Maritimes. And the two of them were safe for the time being. He relaxed a bit. "So why are you calling me? Looking for an update?"

"We already heard about Patel, and the special prosecutor being appointed," Davis told him. "I'm calling because we need you to run a licence plate."

"Oh?"

"Strangers stand out up here. That's why I'm keeping Waddington and Bolton at the cabin—"

"You took Bolton?"

Davis smiled at the alarm in Lossan's voice. The big corporal had always had a soft spot for the Boy Scout. "It was his choice. He got his family out of town and decided to come with us."

Lossan had a hard time believing it was Bolton's choice. He was clenching and unclenching his jaw. He didn't like the thought of his friend mixed up in such a dangerous situation.

"Anyway," Davis continued, "Henry Feathers saw a stranger at the local restaurant. Said the guy looked like a real dirtbag."

"Who is this Henry Feathers?"

"Someone I trust."

Lossan rolled his eyes. "Fine. Give me the licence number."

A few moments later, Lossan was back on the phone. "Okay, the vehicle belongs to a guy name Slattery, address in Burnaby." Lossan touched his chin with his hand. "Slattery … why do I know that name?"

"An ex-con maybe?"

"Don't know," Lossan said, sounding distracted. "He could just be a guy driving through the area. But I'll check him out. Give me your number."

"I'm at a pay phone," Davis told him. "I don't have a landline up here." He checked his watch. "It's almost three. I'll call you tomorrow morning. And Lossan—"

"I know. Don't tell anyone where you are."

Davis hung up the pay phone and scanned the motel parking lot. There were three cars, and the oldest one had the licence plate Henry had given him. It looked like it had been through a war zone. The muffler was hanging low, and it had clearly been in at least one minor accident. Davis walked over to it and peeked in the windows. The inside was a pigsty. There were empty beer cans on the floor in the back seat and wrappers everywhere—and what looked like a file folder shoved under the front seat. Davis glanced around. It was broad daylight, but the place was deserted, and he was out of sight of the restaurant windows. He was looking around for something to break the window when something occurred to him. He tried the door, and it opened.

Davis shook his head and snatched the file folder. There was a single sheet of paper inside.

Chapter 39

After Lossan hung up with Davis, he put in a call to a guy he knew in Drugs. He left a message asking if the name Slattery rang any bells, then set the phone down and stared out the window, thinking about everything going on, particularly his friends isolated in a cabin way up north. They were no nearer finding out who was responsible for Patel's murder, but Slattery might be a lead. If he was involved, they might find out who was pulling the strings. They needed to draw that guy out into the open. Lossan had a hunch it was Alarez. Maybe the Mexican was more important in the cartel's organization than they'd realized.

After a while, Lossan picked up the phone. He needed to bring Boyko up to speed. He wondered how much he could tell him and where it would go. How did the guy handle all the politics? He'd never had the patience.

Boyko listened patiently as Lossan told him he'd been in contact with Davis, though he'd promised not to reveal his location. Boyko sighed at this part but told the corporal to continue. Lossan told him about Slattery. "It could be nothing…"

"You're running it down?"

Lossan hesitated, then said what was really on his mind. "Sir, we can't rule out a connection between the lottery corp and Patel's murder…"

"The lottery corporation has a lot at stake, but I can't believe they'd resort to murder," Boyko replied.

Lossan grimaced. "It's hard to believe they'd go after Waddington either. But someone might be feeding the cartel info, and that's just as bad. It might have got Patel murdered."

"It sounds like Mr. Davis's mistrust of people has rubbed off on you."

Lossan couldn't disagree. "So where does this lead us?"

"Now that the guts of the thing have been laid out in that newspaper article, things might move quickly."

"Any idea where the leak came from, sir?"

"First things first," Boyko said, sidestepping the question. "My superiors in Ottawa want this mess cleaned up. They're worried about the political fallout. It doesn't just put the government in a bad light, but the force as well."

Lossan could feel his face getting hot. So Boyko was a politician after all. "So we just go round in circles?"

"No, Corporal. I'm just telling you what's coming down the pipe. What I and my staff do about it is another matter."

Lossan bit his lip. "Sir … what about … the involvement of … someone else … in the investigation?"

"One of *my* guys you mean. Hard to believe but I guess I can't rule it out." Boyko sighed. "It's difficult to know who to trust these days."

Lossan grunted. "Davis would say not to trust anyone."

"Does that apply to you and me?"

"I'd say so."

There was a period of silence between the two men.

"How do you know I'm not involved?" Boyko said seriously.

"That's easy, sir. If you wanted to deep-six this operation, you'd have closed it down at the start. No one would have questioned that decision. But you didn't."

Chapter 40

A bang startled Slattery. He'd been sitting on the edge of the motel bed, trying to work up the courage to report in to Alarez. He stared dumbly at the window, still bleary-eyed despite having slept for twenty-four hours. The three cups of coffee he'd just poured down his throat hadn't kicked in yet. With a bit of a groan, he heaved himself upright and shuffled to the window to look out. No one was at his door. He looked up at the sky. A bird probably hit the goddam window. Slattery shook his head and immediately regretted it. He took a seat on the edge of his bed to stop the room from spinning.

When he could see again, he looked at his watch. Damn. He had to check out Davis's property. More important, he had to report in to Alarez. He was already a day late. He looked around the dingy motel room, grabbed his coat and took a few tries to get his arm in the sleeve. Finally, he zipped it up and grabbed his keys from the table.

When he opened the door, he anticipated a gust of cold air. What he didn't expect was the fist that slammed into his nose, knocking him backwards into the room. The door shut behind the stranger who'd stepped inside, and then Slattery heard the unmistakable click of a gun cocking.

Through the pain, he blinked a few tears away and gazed up at a large bald man in a black leather jacket standing over him. Slattery's breath caught in his throat. There was a Glock pointed right at his chest.

...

Bolton was never able to sleep well away from his wife, but a nap was now out of the question. He felt on edge with Davis gone.

In the kitchen, Henry and Waddington were still playing cribbage. Bolton put on the kettle and sat down to watch the game.

"You look like you could use some sleep," Waddington commented.

"I could tell you the same thing," Bolton said. "You were up at the crack of dawn. I heard you banging about the kitchen before the sun was up."

Waddington chuckled. "I'm usually up early. It gives me time to think. Besides, I heard you banging around in your bedroom late last night."

Bolton sighed. "I couldn't sleep. I was coming out to get a book and tripped over that bloody chair in the room. It's a tight enough squeeze. Why on earth leave the chair there?"

Henry laughed. "You both have cabin fever," he said. "It's barely been a week. You might be stuck out here for a month."

Bolton stood up to get the kettle. "You know what I hate the most?"

"Yeah," said Waddington. "The waiting."

Bolton poured a touch of boiling water into his tea mug, dumped it and added a fresh bag. Then he filled it with boiling water and covered it with a plate.

"You know what I hate most?" Waddington asked.

"The weather," the other two answered at the same time.

Waddington shared a smile. "Yup. And that's only going to get worse."

"It's winter and we're in the middle of the bush," Bolton said. "I guess that's a good thing. Anyone coming after us will have to drive. We'll see them coming up the driveway."

"Maybe," Waddington said. "But these guys are desperate. They may decide to come in on foot through the bush."

"They might be surprised if they do," Henry said.

"What are you on about?" asked Bolton.

Henry shook his head. "What do you think Alan's been doing the past few days, going out around the property for hours?"

Waddington assumed it was some kind of perimeter check. It was obvious that Bolton thought the same. Neither of them had enough warm clothing or proper boots to spend much time outdoors. It turned out, they both had bigger feet than Davis.

"He's been setting traps," Henry said. "That's one of the reasons he's been telling you not to leave the cabin without him. Doesn't want you to walk right into one."

"What kind of traps?" Bolton was genuinely interested, and he was also feeling a little better knowing that Davis hadn't left them vulnerable. Of course he hadn't. Bolton sat down with his tea and took an Oreo.

"Motion sensors and tripwires," Henry said. "They're connected to radio transmitters that send a signal to that receiver over there." Henry pointed to a side shelf in the kitchen. Bolton hadn't noticed the small black box with an antenna.

"And it makes sense," Henry continued. "Whoever's after you, if they find you, well, they're most likely to come through the bush. With rifles. Probably set fire to the cabin and force you out into the open."

Bolton stopped drinking his tea. When Henry saw the expression on his face, he touched the other man's arm gently. "That's why Alan set perimeter traps, remember? If anyone's coming through the woods, you'll know it, long before they get here."

Henry and Waddington resumed their crib game, and Bolton started to read a book he'd found. It was a history of the area. He stopped when he heard a noise. He stood with his eyes fixed on the front window. "There's a truck…"

"It's Davis," Henry said, recognizing the sound of the truck's engine.

The truck stopped and they saw Davis get out with his gun drawn. Waddington stood as well and was going to sound the alarm, but Henry was already at the front door, shotgun in his hands. He opened it and stood in his socks on the porch, watching as Davis walked around the truck to the passenger side. The truck door creaked open, and a sixty-something man almost fell out into the snow. Davis used his gun to motion him toward the cabin.

Henry backed into the house with his shotgun pointed at the man as he slipped across the drive and stumbled up the stairs and through the door. He didn't look like much of a threat. But Henry waited for Alan's signal before he lowered his gun.

"This is Slattery," Davis told them. "He's the crooked cop who's been working with Alarez."

Chapter 41

Lossan was hungry. He'd started at six that morning and decided he'd head home earlier than usual. He couldn't wait to have his wife's homemade lasagna. He was just leaving his office when the phone rang. Reluctantly he picked it up. It was the detective he'd called about Slattery.

"Yeah, I know the guy," Sloane said. "Used to be a cop. Left the force a few years ago. And not by choice if you get my meaning."

Lossan felt his stomach drop. "What happened?"

"Let's just say, he was involved in too many failed drug busts," Sloane said. "They never could pin anything on him. A few years back, a drug bust went sideways and Slattery's partner was badly beaten. The guy almost died. When the bust went down, Slattery was nowhere to be found. Claimed he didn't know who did it. The investigation was inconclusive. It wasn't the first time things had got screwed up. They figured the guy was on the take but could never prove anything. It got to the point where no one would work with him. Eventually he was told he was done. Supposedly, they cut some sort of deal, but everybody knows the truth—he was forced to leave."

"Thanks, Sloane," Lossan said and quickly hung up. Davis was right. The guy was bad news. And by now, he'd probably told his contact where Waddington and the others were. Lossan picked up the phone again and quickly made another call.

...

Slattery was a font of information. He confirmed he'd been ordered by Alarez to track down Waddington. He smiled when he told Davis that it didn't take him long to find out about his cabin up north and guessed it was a likely hide out. He claimed he'd told the Mexican that heading up north to go after Waddington was a stupid idea. But he wouldn't listen.

Slattery was putting on a brave face. Davis doubted that the bent cop had told the Mexican his plan was stupid.

Davis told the others he'd considered forcing the ex-cop to leave a message for Alarez saying the cabin was a dead end, but decided there was no point. "By now he's probably already on his way."

This made Bolton stop with his mug halfway to his lips. "Should we do something? Should we leave?"

"Where would you go?" Henry asked.

Waddington nodded. "I know it's a risk … but I'm not keen on being on the run. I like to do things on my own terms. Besides … have you seen the weapons in the garage?"

Davis smirked as he led Slattery out of the room. He zip-tied him to a chair in one of the bedrooms and shut the door. When he returned to the kitchen, Bolton looked pale but calm. Davis joined him and the others at the small table and they all tucked into their steak.

"You do realize you kidnapped Slattery, don't you?" Bolton said after a few moments. "That's a rather serious crime."

"What are you talking about? I asked him nicely to come with me and my gun."

Waddington smiled. His admiration for Davis was growing by the day. This ex-con was going out of his way to keep him alive.

Davis took a sip of water. It was getting late. The sun had set, and the stars and a sliver of moon would soon light up the snowy ground.

Bolton cleared his throat and set his knife and fork down on the side of his plate. "Look, I know you don't want to run … but has anyone considered getting some help?" They all stared at him. "I understand you don't trust the police, but do you honestly believe the RCMP detachment up here is tied to the cartel?"

"He's got a point, Davis," Waddington said. "A little help couldn't hurt."

Davis sighed. They were probably right. "But that would mean one of us would have to go to the pay phone in town. There are only four of us as it is." He looked at Bolton. "Three who know how to use a gun."

Bolton was about to stand when Henry put his hand on his shoulder and got up from the table. "I'll do it. I can be back in under an hour."

The idea of getting Henry out of the way was appealing. His friend had already done so much for them. Davis didn't want to put him at any more risk. "Okay, Henry," Davis said. "But make the call and then wait for the cops instead of coming straight back here. There's no point in—"

"I'm coming right back," Henry said. He walked over to the door and started pulling on his boots.

Davis shook his head. "No. It's too dangerous and—"

Henry put a hand up. "You'd do the same for me, Alan."

Davis couldn't argue with that.

Henry pulled on his coat and was just reaching for his shotgun when a loud beep-beep sounded.

Everyone froze—except for Davis, who swung his head toward the receiver on the kitchen shelf. A blue light was flashing. "The west side," he said.

"Could it be an animal?" Waddington asked.

Before Davis answered, the alarm changed to one long beep, and the light flashed red. "And that's the east side," Davis said.

Bolton stood up. "We're surrounded."

Slattery must have been listening to them because he started shouting from behind the bedroom door, "What the hell's going on? Is it Alarez? Don't leave me here!"

"Get your shoes on," Davis said to the others. He got up and headed into the living room where several weapons had been carefully leaned against the wall. He looked at his watch. "We have five minutes. Bolton, cut Slattery loose. Waddington, grab your weapons. Let's move."

For the next several moments, the men moved quickly and silently, getting their gear together. In less than a minute, they were out the door. Davis, Bolton and Slattery headed to the barn where Bolton zip-tied Slattery to some metal pipes by the generator. Henry and Waddington were on a small hill on the other side of the driveway, hidden behind a woodshed.

Barely a minute later, flashlights could be seen heading to the cabin. Davis counted four, two on each side. The lights were aimed low, no doubt in the hopes of avoiding detection. They watched the assailants struggling through the woods, occasionally tripping on the snow-covered undergrowth. Davis smiled. They didn't know they'd hit the tripwires.

Two men stood at the side of the cabin, and two crouched on the porch. One of these slammed his weapon into the window, shattering the glass. Then he tossed something inside.

"Look away!" Davis hissed. His instincts were correct. The flash-bang grenade exploded—the sound was deafening, but their eyes were protected. After a moment, they could look again. Two of the assailants were inside the cabin now, and a short burst of machine gun fire was followed by another and then silence.

Davis flicked a switch just outside the barn. The larger generator began to hum, drawing the attention of the hit men outside. They were confused, squinting into the dim light toward the noise. Davis gambled they'd stay in place, waiting for orders from their leader and not come to investigate in the ten seconds the generator needed to start up. He was right.

Suddenly the power kicked in and searchlights lit up the cabin and the sky above. The place was bathed in light. The two hit men standing outside almost fell backwards in surprise. A third came out of the front door with his weapon up, yelling something Davis couldn't hear over the roar of the generator. The two outside turned and ran up the steps and into the cabin.

Inside, Alarez had ducked down when the light flashed through the cabin windows. They'd been ambushed. He swore under his breath as he crawled along the floor and pulled back part of the curtain in one of the bedrooms at the back of the cabin. But all he could see was bright blinding light. He dropped the curtain and crouched against the wall. Maybe they could knock out the searchlights. He crawled back into the kitchen where the other three men were looking rather lost, holding their weapons against their bodies and huddled in one corner.

The constant loud droning of the generator made it difficult to think. Alarez shouted as loud as he could over the noise. "Take out the goddam lights!"

Suddenly shots were fired through a window at the back of the cabin. The hit men dove to the ground and lay prone. More shots came through windows at the front.

"We're surrounded!" one shouted.

A small cannister came flying in through the broken window. Alarez knew what it was, but didn't have time to move before the smoke began pouring out, blinding them. He covered most of his face with a tea towel from the oven door, coughing and choking on the fumes.

The three hit men gave up their fight with the smoke and poured out of the cabin. They were immediately flanked by Waddington and Davis, who were twenty feet from the porch, and Henry in the driveway. All had weapons pointed at the men. The hit men were still hacking on the fumes and blinded by the searchlight. Trying to shoot out the light was hopeless. Davis barked at them to drop their weapons. All three slowly lowered their weapons and placed them on the porch.

With his shotgun still pointed at them, Davis directed them down the steps toward Henry and Bolton, who was looking uncomfortable with a shotgun in his hands. Waddington kept his shotgun aimed at the front door of the cabin.

"Move," Henry said, following them to the barn.

"Where's the last guy?" Waddington shouted to Davis. Smoke was still coming out the front door and window. They couldn't see anything inside the cabin, and both were squatting low, with weapons up.

Suddenly there came a short burst of machine gun fire from inside the cabin. Waddington was hit in the arm and stumbled backwards. Davis fired through the window and then ducked to the side of the cabin. At the sound of gunfire, Bolton, thirty feet away, instinctively jumped toward the side of the barn and the hit men sprang forward. Henry kept his cool and shot at the ground in front of them, then aimed his shotgun at one of them. They stopped in their tracks and put their hands over their heads.

"Lie face down on the ground. Hands behind your backs where we can see them," Henry yelled. The men hit the ground. Bolton took a breath to calm his nerves, then zip-tied their hands.

Near the porch, Waddington was covering his wound with his hand. It wasn't deep, but he was bleeding a lot.

"Stay there and keep down," Davis said. He crept around the side of the house to the back door, pulling a bandana over his mouth and nose. Through the crack in the door, he saw movement in the kitchen. Alarez was slithering across the floor. Smoke lingered in the hall, and his eyes started watering, but the bandana kept him from coughing.

Davis aimed just above Alarez's head and fired a warning shot.

Alarez stopped and rolled over, groaning as he aimed his weapon at Davis. He was clearly injured. Davis waited. Nothing was more dangerous than a wounded animal.

"Give up now, and I'll let you live," Davis called. "You don't let go of the gun, I'll shoot you dead."

Alarez was trying to hold his side and hang on to his gun. Sticky blood covered his fingers, and he was so tired. He just wanted to see his family again. "I surrender," he said. "Just … I just want to see my wife and son."

Davis peeked in. Alarez had dropped his weapon and was lying on his side, holding his wound with both hands. Davis kept his weapon trained on him as he slowly moved forward. But he needn't have worried, by the time he got there, Alarez had passed out.

A few minutes later, with the large generator turned off, an eerie silence descended over the snowy landscape, now lit only by the stars and moon. The three hit men were seated on the frozen ground with Bolton watching over them.

"They won't talk," Bolton said when Davis walked over.

The men were seated on the ground, their backs against the barn, their hands tied behind them and their legs outstretched. Davis pulled out a large hunting knife.

"Bloody hell," Bolton muttered from behind him. Davis crouched down and stared at the one closest to him.

"Your name?" Davis asked.

"Piss off."

In one swift movement, Davis stabbed the hunting knife into the ground three inches from the man's groin. The man yelled and tried to jump back, but there was nowhere to go. Davis pressed the blade against the man's thigh and twisted it, drawing blood and a scream from his victim.

"Now, let's try again. Which of you is Alarez?"

"In the cabin! The guy in the cabin."

For the next few minutes, Davis questioned them, but it was clear that these were low-level hired hands. They really didn't know anything more than Alarez's name.

"Well, "Davis said, "looks like it's time to question Alarez." He turned and headed toward the cabin.

Bolton sat on a large log and tried to take it all in. He felt sick at the way Davis dealt with the hit men, but he had to admit, he got results.

"I better go call the police," said Henry, walking toward him with Waddington by his side, cradling his arm.

Suddenly Bolton heard what he thought were sirens. Headlights were coming through the bush along the dirt road as the sirens got louder.

Two RCMP cruisers pulled in by the barn and came to a stop. Four officers from the Anahim Lake RCMP detachment got out of their vehicles and surveyed the scene.

"Which one of you is Davis?" one asked.

Bolton pointed toward the front porch where Davis was standing over Alarez.

"How on earth did you find us?' Bolton asked.

"We got a call from Vancouver," said the officer in charge. "From a Corporal Lossan. Said his friends were up here and needed help."

Chapter 42

As they waited for the ambulance, Alarez had time to think. The attack on Waddington had failed. Slattery was a useless blubbering idiot who seemed bent on telling the police everything he knew.

Alarez, on the other hand, didn't have a choice. He had to make a deal.

"You know you have a crooked cop on your team," he said.

They all looked at each other.

"I want to make a deal. And then I'll tell you who warned me to disappear. And who's been taking money for years to help our operation."

Bolton surprised them all by jumping forward and demanding, "Who? Who is it?"

"First you get my wife and son out of Mexico. I won't tell you anything if the cartel gets them."

"Just tell us who," Bolton insisted.

But Alarez closed his mouth. He felt safe from Davis and the others with the RCMP there. And he knew he had information they desperately wanted. But first, he would protect his family.

Fifteen minutes later, three ambulances pulled up. Alarez was treated and considered stable enough to make the trip to the Cariboo Memorial Hospital in Williams Lake. Three RCMP officers would accompany Alarez and the other hit men to hospital and keep guard until they were relocated to Vancouver.

Davis, Bolton, Henry and Waddington followed the RCMP officer in charge to the Anahim detachment.

Back at the detachment, Slattery was placed in a cell, and the officer in charge took each of them for questioning. When three of them suggested he contact a Superintendent Boyko with RCMP Security Services in Vancouver, the officer relented. After making a call to Boyko, the officer was satisfied that under the circumstances, no charges would be laid and he released them all. Slattery would be transferred to Vancouver in the morning.

Davis then contacted Lossan and made him promise to keep quiet about Alarez being in custody until they knew the name of the dirty cop.

"Except for Boyko," Lossan said. "You're going to have to trust my instincts on this, he's a good man."

Davis was silent for a moment, then he said, "It's your call."

...

The call from DEA agent Carlos Adriano came less than an hour later.

"We have Alarez's wife and son in custody," Adriano said. "The Mexican police arrested them and handed them over at the border crossing in El Paso."

Lossan felt his jaw loosen. "That's a relief," he said. "Thank you, Carlos. We'll tell Alarez. He'll want to speak to them."

"Of course. When you are ready, we'll arrange a call."

...

According to the attending doctor at Cariboo Memorial hospital, Alarez was a lucky man. Davis's bullet had gone clean through his lower abdomen and missed everything important. The wound was cleaned and patched, and there was no internal bleeding.

"Good," Waddington said gingerly. "He'll be back in the cells in Vancouver in no time."

...

At 8:00 a.m. Lossan walked through the double doors at the end of the hallway of the hospital where Alarez was being guarded by the two RCMP officers. A very serious-looking Boyko told Lossan he wanted to talk to Alarez on his own. Lossan nodded and walked over to greet the others and hear all about what happened at the cabin. Boyko went into Alarez's room and shut the door.

"Mr. Alarez, we finally meet. You may not be aware of this, but we've been working on a joint operation with Commercial Crime and the DEA."

Alarez shrugged. "I told the others; I will say nothing until I know my wife and son are safe."

"Your wife and son are safe for now. The DEA picked them up early this morning and escorted them back to the US."

Alarez smiled. "You pigs are stupid. Now that they are safe, do you think I will tell you anything?"

Boyko smiled back. "Mr. Alarez, you seem to be under the impression that we're keeping your family safe for you. Let me explain what's going on. We're holding your family as leverage against you. If you don't tell us exactly what we want to know, they'll be shipped back to Mexico immediately."

Alarez tried to sit but he winced in pain. "You are lying."

"Would you like to find out?"

Alarez looked like he could spit nails, but Boyko didn't flinch. He was used to getting under guys' skin. "Especially when we leak the story that you're cooperating with us," Boyko continued smoothly. "That you've told us all about your dealer network and the names of your contacts in Mexico. They'll want to punish you. And if they can't punish you, well…"

Alarez spluttered but Boyko silenced him with a glare.

Alarez stared at his hands on the white bedsheets. *This is Canada, surely they can't do this*, he thought. Cops didn't threaten people like that here.

"The point is, you either cooperate fully or we'll have no reason to hold your family. We will have to release them, and they'll take their chances."

Alarez was quiet for a long moment. Then he said, "I'll cooperate, but first I want to speak to my wife."

"I thought you might," said Boyko.

Chapter 43

A week later, Boyko hosted a dinner in the private dining room of a high-end Vancouver steak house. Despite things moving forward, when Bolton walked in, he felt a heaviness in the room. There were people missing. He was sad for Charlie Patel, and for Ed Landy and his wife. He recently discovered that Bob's boss had not been involved in the money laundering. When Bolton alerted him to the possibility of something illegal going on, Landy had started an investigation and was subsequently threatened by Alarez. When he left town, Alarez had him murdered to ensure there were no loose ends.

Lossan was talking quietly with Holliday in the corner of the dining room. At the table, Davis had already taken a seat and was drinking scotch. He looked more like a biker than ever, with faded jeans and a black leather jacket. Lossan wasn't sure how he'd gotten in. The restaurant had made it clear to him when he booked the room that they had a strict dress code and there were no exceptions.

Two well-dressed waiters circulated the room serving twelve-year-old Barolo.

Waddington was leaning over the long table, helping himself to some appetizers. Boyko glanced at his watch and then cleared his throat as if to get everyone's attention. He decided to wait until they were all there.

A moment later, the door opened and Cameron walked in. One of the waiters offered him a glass of wine.

Boyko stood up and walked to the end of the table. "Corporal Lossan and I thought we should have a dinner to celebrate capturing Alarez," he said, "and to bid farewell to our friend Charlie Patel, a good cop who lost his life in the line of duty." His face darkened. "And you all deserve an explanation." His eyes met Davis's, but there were no I-told-you-so's from the ex-gangster. "You were right, Mr. Davis. We had a crooked cop right here on our team."

Boyko looked around at them all. "We brought Tom Haddock in last week. With Alarez's information, there was no point in his holding back. He told me everything." Boyko shook his head and took a breath. "I want you all to know, he really meant what he said that first day. For a lot of years, Tom did everything he could to expose what was going on, to get drugs off our streets and take down the guys running it all."

"What happened?" Bolton hadn't meant to say it out loud, but in the emptiness, he felt bewildered. How did someone good become so bad?

"He saw too much and couldn't do anything about it," Davis said.

Boyko nodded. "That was a big part of it, yes. Tom was working with informants and witnesses, and every day the money and drugs kept pouring in, and the money laundering continued. He reported it over and over again. But nothing ever happened. He saw the cartels and their high-priced lawyers just getting richer.

"And then he took that damn bullet. After that, he was a changed man. It felt like he gave up. I just thought…" Boyko shook his head. "None of us realized how much he was struggling."

"And it would have been easy," Cameron said from the other side of the room, "what with Tom always working with senior gang members."

"He made a choice," Davis said. "Lots of cops take bullets. They see the shit that goes down and they can't fix it all. But they don't decide to become part of it. None of *you* did."

Lossan looked around the room and his eyes settled on Boyko. He raised his glass. "To lost friends," he said.

"To Charlie," Boyko added.

And they drank silently to their friend.

...

Jani Stuart hadn't heard from Bolton in months and was surprised by his visit that evening. He'd aged and looked tired.

"I've got news," he said gently. "You were right about Bob. He didn't leave you on purpose. He would never have done that. And now we have the proof."

Jani started to cry. "I'll never be able to thank you enough. You were always such a good friend to us."

She hugged him, and he could feel her trembling in his arms. It was finally over, and she could move on with her life.

...

Boyko had let Slattery cool his heels for a few nights in a downtown cell. The ex-cop hadn't been sober in years. When he was brought into an interview room the following morning, he reiterated all he'd told the others in the cabin.

Lossan thought it was like watching someone wring out an old wet rag. There was just nothing left inside the guy. He wondered if Slattery knew or would even care that he was just four blocks from the war zone of the Downtown Eastside, where addicts lived on the streets, sex workers disappeared without a trace and hustlers exchanged cash for drugs in broad daylight—and largely because of people like him helping the cartel bring drugs into the city. Somehow, it was little consolation that he'd be going to prison. It seemed to Lossan like he'd been there for years already.

Chapter 44

A letter of understanding was signed between Crown counsel, US counsel for the DEA and Alarez's lawyer. Alarez confirmed that the cartel had been laundering their drug money through the casinos using the triad. He told them about the network of local contractors who met the vessels offshore in high-powered speed boats and gave them details of shipments they made over the last three months.

Back at Heather Street, Lossan told the DEA that Alarez claimed the cartel had triad connections in four major US cities and gave them the names of guys that managed those relationships. It was enough for Adriano to call the FBI, who decided to start an investigation of EFT Bank in the States as well as Bitale Bank in Mexico.

FBI agents flew to Vancouver and met with Lossan, Holliday and Superintendent Boyko. Within two weeks, EFT Bank in Vancouver was forced to sign a cooperation agreement with the RCMP Security Services and granted access to all bank records and full cooperation of all their staff.

Over the next several weeks, the RCMP raided over a dozen underground casinos, including three private residences and casinos located inside Chinese restaurants predominantly in the Richmond and Kingsway areas. In one mansion, surrounded by walls and lush gardens in the exclusive Shaughnessy neighbourhood, police discovered four Asian women chained to walls in the cellar. The women's heads were shaved, they were naked and malnourished, and they had been sexually assaulted. There was no toilet in the basement and the floors were covered in human feces. Dog bowls of drinking water sat next to the soiled mattresses they were forced to sleep on.

At first they refused to speak to anybody. An interpreter was brought in, and when she explained that they had been rescued by police officers, they decided to talk.

Two of them were members of a group of sex trade workers who'd been in the country for three months. The other two had been employed in the gambling industry. One had worked in Macau and came to Vancouver with the promise of a job in a major casino. While acting as a croupier in an underground casino, she was also used to handing out money to whales at different casinos. She'd lost money gambling and been held prisoner until she could repay her debts. She'd borrowed from the wrong people.

The Shaughnessy and Richmond homes were registered in the name of numbered companies tied to members of various Macau-based triads. A few were Canadian residents. The police arrested several individuals. Two turned out to be mid-level Chinese government officials with known triad connections, and one was on China's most wanted list. There was an outstanding extradition order against him.

Under the special powers granted to the police, the restaurants and homes that were raided were shut down and boarded up. The police embarked on the slow process of putting the properties up for sale as proceeds of crime. They doubted the registered owners would be in a hurry to contact them.

· · ·

A flurry of newspaper articles told the world about the casino problem in Vancouver and the Canadian government's lack of action. Canada had become a haven for organized crime, and it seemed a lot of people knew about the rotting corpses beneath the glitz and glamour of the casinos. Now the stench was bubbling up through cracks that were slowly widening.

The premier of BC announced that two assistant deputy ministers and a mid-level bureaucrat had been put on paid leave pending a government investigation. And there were rumours that she'd asked for the resignations of both the finance minister and the attorney general. When she claimed she had no knowledge of the money laundering inside the casinos, there were howls of laughter. A few days later, the headline in the *Vancouver Sun* read like an epitaph: "We don't believe you, goodbye."

Despite her appointment of a retired criminal judge to head up a public enquiry, she was called on to resign.

The premier was forced to call an election, and the opposition party formed a new government. It claimed that hundreds of millions of dollars had been laundered through BC casinos on an annual basis for almost a decade. Waddington knew it was much more. He was commissioned to make recommendations on eliminating money laundering inside BC casinos.

He took less than two weeks to deliver his report, which recommended reduced betting limits, barring loan sharks and people with a criminal record, and eliminating the use of cash inside the casinos. The new government wasn't happy with Waddington's report. Like its predecessor, it was afraid of losing casino revenues.

But they appointed Waddington as the new CEO of the lottery corporation.

...

The US Department of Justice sued EFT Bank in Canada and its US subsidiary and pushed for their closure. The Canadian government decided that since the two countries had just announced a joint strategy on organized crime, this wasn't the time to go to bat for a mid-sized bank. They forced it to be sold.

Boyko avoided getting directly involved in the joint task force on organized crime. He and his number two worked on a briefing paper that was shared with their US counterparts. He wasn't a fan of editing out the truth, and this wasn't the time to hold back. He knew it wouldn't take long for his superiors to figure out where the information had come from. But Boyko was bulletproof. He knew which government departments and ministers had held back or even suppressed critical information that had been hidden from both the Canadian public and their US allies. He also knew which press conferences had been cancelled at the last minute because of government fears that announcing massive drug busts of triads who had ties to the Chinese government might upset China. He'd done his thirty years; his pension was safe.

The joint strategy on organized crime published a report that recommended, among other things, an annual national security report on illicit trade and the development of a North America–wide approach to target drug trafficking and other organized crime.

Boyko wondered how many of these recommendations would see the light of day and how many would die because of the lack of political will. He started thinking about retirement. Despite all the talk, things were moving too slowly.

Epilogue

Eighteen months later

Boyko had retired from the RCMP and joined a private consulting firm advising governments, large corporations and NGOs on transnational crime, national security and corruption.

On a warm day in June, he met Davis in the parking lot of a sky train station in Burnaby. "I hope you don't mind, but we're going to Richmond."

Davis had been living up north at his cabin. He and Henry were renovating it—and spending a lot of time playing cribbage in the quiet evenings. He'd never felt so at peace. But he liked a trip to the city occasionally, so when Boyko had contacted him, he'd decided to come.

Boyko was quiet as they drove along Marine Drive and pulled onto the Arthur Laing Bridge toward Richmond. They drove past the River Rock Casino and turned onto Westminster Highway. They passed a mid-level office tower. "That's where Chinese gangsters stockpiled drug cash," Boyko said. "It's the same place Vincent Ramos ran his company. Ever heard of him?"

Davis shook his head.

"He was a cyber genius. Could have had a great career in the tech industry, but he decided to work for criminals. His company sold modified cellphones to organized crime. They couldn't be hacked or wiretapped. The Sinaloa cartel used them to distribute their drugs around the world. Eventually, the FBI got him and a lot of his clients, including some major players in the Sinaloa cartel."

They came across a busy street full of restaurants, currency exchange shops, storefront law firms and travel agencies. Boyko pointed to a massage parlour as they drove past it. "That used to be owned by the Chinese government," he said, "and operated by triads. Drug traffickers would carry suitcases of cash inside. Most would stay long enough to visit the fourteen-year-old masseuses and settle gambling debts."

Farther on, they passed a row of rundown warehouses and storage lockers. "You know how many counterfeit products are stored at places like this? Fake Nikes from China, along with loads of chemical precursors. It's called trade-based finance. The cartel converts its cash for product. A quick phone call and a cash drop is made to a Richmond textile merchant, and a few weeks later, a shipload of Gucci knock-offs arrives in Guangdong."

Boyko shook his head. "Gangsters don't use casinos anymore. They trade drugs for knock-off luxury goods. Crime hasn't gone away, it's just changed."

They pulled into the parking lot of the strip mall. Boyko cut the engine and looked at the restaurant. "Two cops died here. An undercover op gone wrong. They were on the trail of a kingpin importing chemicals from China to make meth here in Vancouver. Intelligence just confirmed the gangsters were connected to Chinese intelligence. The hit was sanctioned by Beijing."

"Why are you telling me all this?" Davis asked.

"I thought you might be interested in joining our team."

Davis smiled. "Nah. I'm too old," he said. "But I know someone who might be."

As Boyko dropped him off, Davis looked at him and said, "One thing I'd like to know."

"What's that?"

"It was you who leaked the story to the press right?"

Boyko just smiled.

Acknowledgements

I'd like to thank my friends Andrew and Jani Basford for their insights into ex-pat life in Hong Kong, my good friend John Hall for reading the manuscript and his comments on the law, and my wife, Daphne, for her keen eye and support throughout. The gang at Iguana were, as always, patient and encouraging, especially Paula Chiarcos.